Ivory's Familiars

MONTANA ASH

Published by Paladin Publishing

Ivory's Familiars
Copyright © 2017 by Montana Ash
Latest update 2023

Cover design by: Covers by Christian
Editing and proofreading by: Messenger's Memos – Fiction
Editing Services
Formatting by: Montana Ash

All rights reserved.

Ivory's Familiars

MONTANA ASH

Dedication

*I dedicate Vaughn, Seth, Ronan, and Ivory to all my
wonderfully naughty readers who demanded – I mean,
suggested – I give reverse harem a whirl.
Thank you.
This one's for you!*

Author's Note

This book contains sexually explicit material between three men and one woman in a reverse harem/polyamorous relationship and is only intended for adults. It is a standalone with no cliffhanger and a guaranteed happily ever after.

One

nother bar. Another town. Another shitty job,
Seth thought, raising the dark ale to his
lips and taking a healthy swallow.

Sometimes his resentment over his current situation got to him. He had a purpose, and it wasn't that of a travelling vagrant. But, he supposed, if he was ever going to find what he was looking for, then he had to keep moving – and working. If he didn't work, he didn't get paid. And if he didn't get paid, he and his colleagues couldn't afford the constant travel, endless dreary bars, and craptastic takeaway meals they subjected their bodies to daily. He knew the others had pretty much given up on their original mission, thinking the chances of finding what they sought decreased as the years went by. But he believed the opposite; the more places they eliminated, the closer they got to finding the right one.

So, although his soul yearned to fulfil its true purpose, he contented himself with his current day job – a bodyguard for hire. They weren't due to meet their newest client until the following day, thus their current location. Not that it bothered him. They were seated in a booth in a surprisingly homey and clean bar. If he wasn't mistaken, the seats were real leather in an appealing deep burgundy that set off the rich tones in the darkly stained wooden table tops. The flooring was real stonework in a mixture of greys, blues, and pale green, with the walls being an unusual mix of exposed brick, interspersed with artwork and artefacts.

The large bar stretched in an elegant horseshoe shape and featured more of those real stones as the base and a smooth, shiny, dark granite for the top. Tall stools lined the bar, and tables were spread out evenly in the spacious area, bypassing where the solo pool table, jukebox, and small stage were situated. Six booths on either side of the room completed the seating arrangements and were already quite full even though it wasn't yet six in the evening, indicating the small, out-of-the-way bar in the middle of the mountains was quite popular. To Seth's mind, it was the perfect combination of modern and rustic charm. He also approved of the name: The Hex Bar. It was the whole reason why he had chosen this particular establishment . . . and also the reason why Vaughn was currently brooding into his Guinness in the corner.

Vaughn didn't have much of a sense of humour – but Seth was working on that. However, given that he had known the other man for over ten years now and had seen little to no comedic improvement in that time, he figured his chances of success were minute. Seth didn't really mind. He happened to find the broody look rather attractive. Actually, he found everything about the man attractive, from his dirty-blond hair, bright-green eyes, and chiselled jawline, down to his broad shoulders, tapered waist, and size twelve feet. And really, his temperamental personality and surly attitude were more than compensated by Ronan – his other colleague.

Although not as outwardly friendly or flirtatious as himself, Ronan was at least a decent conversationalist – and easy-going to boot. His boy-next-door good looks of green eyes, messy brown hair, dimpled cheeks and a six-foot-one tightly muscled frame made him one delicious package of maleness. His own appearance wasn't too shabby – *even if I say so myself*, Seth thought. He was tall and ripped, with short black hair . . . and green eyes. The green eyes were a shared trait amongst the three of them, although they were all slightly different in their tones, with Vaughn's being the brightest and his being the darkest. Ronan's were a happy medium between them – much like his personality.

The green eyes were pretty much a given for his kind and the three of them were often mistaken for brothers because of them – a fact that always creeped him out given their sleeping arrangements. They were witches' familiars who shared their spirit with the black panther – or black jaguar, to be exact. Hence, their feline green eyes – and all that purring during the night. Nope, no tame little black house cats as human law would have everyone believe. The three of them were predators, pure and simple, and born to protect and aid the witches of the world. Thus, Seth's amusement, Ronan's resignation, and Vaughn's anger over the name of the bar. They knew all too well that hexes were in fact real, and that's exactly what had Seth pushing a loudly protesting

Vaughn, and an eye-rolling Ronan into the drinking establishment only ten minutes prior.

Okay, so maybe it was in poor taste, but Seth had to get his kicks somewhere. And given his buddies insisted on going out for drinks instead of spending the evening in their dinky hotel room as he had voted for, he had stubbornly insisted on this watering hole for the evening.

"This place is nice, huh?" he asked his companions cheerily.

Vaughn's response was typically non-verbal; he frowned deeply in the direction of the artwork on the wall next to their booth – a pentacle – and followed it up with a long drink from the cold glass he held.

Ronan was a wee bit more vocal, admitting, "It's far nicer than most of the places we drink at. You have to give the owner credit for authenticity."

"Authenticity, my arse! There's a fucking cauldron in the corner!" Vaughn declared.

Seth cast his green eyes to the object in question sitting quite happily in the front corner of the room. It was a large, aged-looking iron cauldron, sitting squat on three small but sturdy legs. A sign in a fancy cursive script above it declared it a 'wishing cauldron,' prompting customers to throw in their spare coins and make a wish. Seth thought it was rather enterprising of the owner and it actually looked quite legit – if witches still used such a thing, of course. Most modern-day witches didn't use big cauldrons like those, but they did use smaller versions in order to mix herbs and such for their spells – particularly hedge witches.

He shrugged. "Well, I think it adds to the overall atmosphere."

Vaughn drained his glass, thunking it noisily onto the table. "Must you always be so happy?" he demanded.

"Must you always be so grumpy?" He smiled back sweetly.

"He wasn't so grumpy this morning when he woke up to my mouth on his dick," Ronan commented, almost idly. "And you weren't so happy when you woke up and my mouth *wasn't* on your dick," he pointed out.

Seth laughed out loud at that, nudging Vaughn with his shoulder when the older man coughed out a laugh too. His grin highlighted his sharp cheekbones and his eyes lightened prettily in his mirth. Vaughn really was a good-looking son of a bitch, and even *he* wasn't immune to the good nature of

Ronan. He was their resident mediator and politician – always knowing the right thing to say and the right time to say it. He was a master at balancing Seth's own perkiness with Vaughn's pigheadedness.

He winked at Ronan, both in thanks for the timely banter and also in flirtation. "Thanks for reminding me that you owe me a blowjob."

Ronan opened and closed his mouth for a moment before shrugging. "It's a hard job, but somebody's gotta do it."

The three of them laughed at the very deliberate pun, and Seth felt them all finally relax. It had been a long drive to the small town at the base of the Seregil mountains and they had just come off another job without any downtime in between. But the woman who had hired them had seemed desperate to get them here as soon as humanly possible. So, they had finished up with their small-time businessman and his psychotic ex-wife just the evening before and had driven the ten hours to Hadleigh in order to meet up with their new mystery client the following day.

Noting everyone's glasses were empty, Seth stood. "I'll get us another round. Same again?" His men nodded, and he stood up, accidentally backing into another patron and spilling some of his brew. "Crap! Sorry about that," he promptly apologised.

The other man swore colourfully, shaking his hand to dislodge the spilled beer. "Watch yourself, kid," he warned angrily, causing Seth to raise his eyebrows over the obvious animosity.

"He said he was sorry."

The words were practically growled out, and if looks could kill, Seth was pretty sure the trashy truckie would be six feet under right about now. But then, Vaughn's scowl could do that to a man. The rude drunk moved on pretty quickly after that, and Seth sent his friend a look he knew was filled with both annoyance and resignation. The look the older man threw back was filled with a whole lot of 'I don't give a fuck.' Sliding his glance to the left, he looked hopefully at Ronan, only to shake his head when he saw that Ronan was also scowling fiercely after the man's retreating back.

Seth sighed; they were a little protective of him. A fact he found endlessly amusing given he topped them both in height and also muscle mass. When he was feeling magnanimous, he could kind of under-stand it. Not only was he the youngest of the three, but he was also the last to join their little trio. Ronan and Vaughn had been in the same coven since before the Salem witch trials in 1692. They had been serving their bloodline side by side for hundreds of years in one form or another before he had even been born. Familiars like himself were always born specifically to one bloodline and although they weren't immortal by any stretch of the imagination, their souls would always return in a new body to be a companion, protector, spy – whatever their witch wanted or needed – to serve a whole new generation of witches. His lovers had been serving the same bloodline for almost ten generations, while Seth was only on his first spin. And truthfully, he was yet to serve anyone, given they hadn't been able to find their witch!

With his fresh first-time soul, they were far more experienced in many ways, hence the overprotectiveness. His shiny new familiar soul did not, however, make him naïve. Hell, he was the one who had convinced them all to move past the 'friend zone' and into the 'screw-like-rabbits zone.' Vaughn and Ronan hadn't even realised they were in love with each other until he had come along. It had taken Seth all of one night in their presence to see the intimate and electric connection between the pair. It had been an unfortunate combination of fear, stubbornness, and pride that had kept them both from acting on their feelings. They were both so close that neither of them had wanted to upset the apple cart by admitting to romantic feelings. On top of that, neither of them had ever been with another man before either. They had both believed themselves to be straight as a ruler – boobies all the way! Seth, having always been into variety, had quickly made them see the error of their ways, and they had all been together very happily on every level for over ten years now.

Definitely not naïve, Seth thought in amusement. He had shown the older pair the many benefits to be had in diversity.

"I'll get those drinks," he stated, returning to the present.

Vaughn stood up. "I'll come with you."

"I don't need a babysitter," he grumbled.

"I need to stretch my legs."

No, you don't, Seth thought. *You want to make sure the big, bad drunk doesn't hurt little 'ole me.* The protectiveness was tiresome . . . but also nice. It was a gift to know you were loved – and not just by one person, but by two. He was a firm believer that love knew no bounds. Love wasn't like a bucket of water that you could fill up; it was limitless and flexible and enduring.

Feeling a little sentimental, he leaned down and pecked a chaste kiss to Vaughn's lips. "Thank you."

Apple-green eyes widened in surprise, but also lit with warmth. "What was that for?"

He shrugged. "Just because I can. I – *oof!*" His breath left him in a rush as he was rudely shoved in the shoulder from behind.

"Bloody fags! Typical!" was the insulting mutter from behind him and he didn't need to turn to know it was the same mouthy drunk from minutes before.

Vaughn, being Vaughn, didn't even bother to comment – or blink – aiming a punch at the drunkard's extended belly. Seth watched him stumble back into the table behind him, wheezing out a breath as he grasped at his gut. At least Vaughn had tempered his strength. If he hadn't, the guy's stomach would have a fist-sized hole in it, and his spine would be on display to the entire bar. Their kind was very strong . . . and very dominant . . . and very possessive. Which was why good-natured Ronan was also on his feet, cracking his knuckles and brushing against Seth's biceps in an attempt to remove the idiot's scent from his skin.

Three men rushed over to the fallen man, helping him to stand upright while glaring daggers in their direction. "What the fuck?" one of them yelled, advancing aggressively towards them.

Uh oh, not good. Seth winced internally. It was never wise to corner a cat.

"We don't want any trouble." Ronan, the peacemaker, held his hands up in supplication. Seth really hoped they listened, for those same hands could twist the heads off these idiots' bodies in the blink of an eye.

The advancing man sneered, "Oh, you don't? Well, you should have thought of that before you attacked my brother!"

"We didn't attack anybody . . ." Ronan tried appeasing the man, but Seth could tell it was going to be in vain. Unfortunately, they ran into these types of ignorant arseholes with alarming regularity. They also found themselves in an alarming number of bar fights.

All four men were now glaring belligerently at them, their postures hostile and their intentions clear to the whole bar given how quiet the large space now was.

"This is going to be fun."

Seth rolled his eyes at Vaughn's muttered words. But even as he took up a defensive stance, he couldn't help the small thrill leaping in his belly. The sex was always stupendous after a good brawl. Vaughn was like a – *ha ha* – animal.

"Excuse me, gentlemen."

The reprimand came from behind them and was as sharp as it was sexy. *Sexy? Where the hell did that come from?* Quickly on the heels of the auditory stimulation came a delicious scent – like thunderstorms and vanilla and freshly turned earth. Three things his panther very much appreciated. Eager to see why his inner animal seemed so interested, he turned to the owner of the voice . . . and was shocked to see an average-looking woman, perhaps in her late twenties, with average-looking brown hair and average clothes. This was the owner of the sexy voice? Not that he had anything against average – he didn't care what people looked like on the outside as much as he cared about how they acted. But the woman's voice was husky, alluring . . . seductive. It was hard to reconcile that voice with the woman standing in front of him.

"No fighting in my establishment, boys. Either take your seats or leave."

Seth shivered. That voice was really working for him, no doubt about that, and he found himself wondering what it sounded like in the midst of passion. Next to him, a loud throat clearing interrupted his unexpectedly lustful and entirely inappropriate thoughts, and he started guiltily, darting a glance towards his lovers. He was shocked to see that they appeared to be just as transfixed as he was ... and just as lustful if the heat coming off them was any indication. What the hell was going on here?

Early in their relationship, they had often invited others to join them in the bedroom. To his mind, multiple partners always added to the enjoyment and experience. But as their relationship had evolved from purely physical pleasure to intimate loving, they had stopped sharing themselves with others. In fact, he hadn't been tempted in years to revisit that part of their past, even though all three of them enjoyed the feel of feminine curves and the sound of feminine sighs. He knew the others felt the same way – what they shared was far too important to jeopardise for a mere roll between the sheets with a stranger. He was quite content never to touch another woman – or man – ever again. So why did the unexceptional woman in front of him stir such dormant desires?

"He started it! He hit me!" the drunk yelled childishly, pointing an accusing finger at Vaughn.

Vaughn merely raised one eyebrow, looking

handsome, bored, and belligerent at the same time – a look only he could pull off.

"I don't particularly care," the sexy-voiced average woman said. "No fighting. Full stop."

"We apologise. We didn't intend to start any trouble," Ronan explained. "We were just leaving," he added, causing Seth to whip his head around and stare at him.

They were not just leaving – they were supposed to be having another drink. Besides, he was now more than a little intrigued, not just with the bar, but also its owner.

He opened his mouth to dispute Ronan's claim, only to close it again when Ronan shook his head. The man was clearly serious about leaving. Sighing, Seth turned to the mysterious woman. "Right. Just leaving. Great place you have here."

The woman smiled, revealing even white teeth. "Thank you. I like it."

"Great name," he added. *What am I doing?* he wondered. Was he stalling for time, creating conversation just so he could hear the woman talk some more? Glancing at Ronan and Vaughn, he saw they were both watching him curiously, and he felt another stab of guilt. His flirting days were supposed to be over. "Anyway, sorry again for the trouble."

Spinning, he forced himself to walk away without looking back – a task that was surprisingly and confusingly difficult. Feeling warmth on either side of him, he knew Ronan and Vaughn had caught up. He had everything he needed and wanted right beside him, he assured himself. So why was there a small traitorous voice inside his head calling his bluff?

Two

I vory waited a full ten seconds after the door closed behind the three strangers to release the breath she had been holding.

Holy cow, talk about sex on legs! Those three men were absolutely spectacular in their virility. All so different in their looks, and yet each one was just as appealing to her, from the tall black-haired one, to the shorter brunette and even the blond broody one. She'd never really had a type per se, and with those three, she figured she didn't need to. She'd just take the trifecta, thank you very much. Shaking her head at her crazed, lustful inner ramblings, she turned and ran headfirst into her head bartender, Lee.

"Geez, I'm sorry, boss. I was just coming to check you were okay. Libby told me there was trouble."

Ivory smiled. Lee was a little overprotective. "It's fine, Lee. Nothing to worry about. One punch – not even what you would call a scuffle."

He frowned, his blue eyes glaring daggers at the door as if daring the troublemakers to come back. "I was on my break in the back. Otherwise I would have been here. I've told you before that we need to hire bouncers for this place. We get so many more lowlifes now that the bypass has closed."

Ivory sighed, pushing past Lee and picking up a stack of dirty glasses on her way back to the bar. The closure of the bypass six months ago had very likely saved her business. Tourists, businessmen, and truckers were now forced to pass through their small town instead of going around it. Business was booming. So much so that she had been able to hire Lee in the first place. Although, he was right about their clientele, which was far more varied than it used to be. As such, there was bound to be the odd troublemaker or two. So far, she and her current staff had been able to handle them easily enough. Besides, she didn't mind a good pub fight once in a while – made the place more authentic.

She hadn't heard or seen what had prompted the large man to sucker punch Trucker Pete, but she figured it was something to do with Pete's foul mouth. Pete was a regular whenever he was on one of his supply runs for his trucking company. Largely, he was well-behaved, but he was a mean drunk when he had too much whiskey in him. If she had been working the bar tonight, she would have cut him off three drinks ago. But she had been in the back working on her accounts – and checking her mail. Something she did rather obsessively these days thanks to her new little pen pal. Not wanting to get caught up in those depressing thoughts once again, she turned to Lee who had followed her back behind the bar;

"We don't need bouncers. They'd ruin the ambience of the place. Besides," she cut him off before he could argue further, "the only reason I stepped in was because those guys would have wiped the floor with Pete and his team and then used them as toothpicks."

And she had no doubt that was true. All three of them were tall – likely a few inches over six feet – far taller than her own five-foot-seven frame. She'd had to raise her head to look them in the eyes – and oh, what magnificent eyes they had been too. Even in the dark interior of the bar, she had been able to see that each of the men had green eyes, albeit in varying shades. Maybe they were brothers? Their postures and familiarity hinted they were close. Whatever they were, they were three of the best specimens she'd had the pleasure of laying her eyes on in years.

"Boss? Ivory!"

"Huh?" She looked up to see Lee frowning at her. Oops, he must have been trying to gain her attention for a while now. *Head back in the game, Ivory. You have enough complications without adding three strange men to the mix.* "I'm sorry, Lee. What did you say?"

"I asked if you were sure you wanted to close up tonight. I can stay back, help out."

Ivory smiled. He really was a good guy – too bad she didn't find him as attractive as those strangers. If she had, she would have taken him up on his offer of a date when he had first started working for her. But he just didn't ring any of her bells. "No, thanks. It's your night to finish early. I'll be fine. Besides, it's already slowing down. I'll be closing up on time," she answered in response to his offer.

Lee nodded, moving back to the front of the bar to serve. He still had one hour left on shift. Pleased that Lee wasn't going to argue with her, she picked up the rack of dirty glasses and walked them back to the kitchen and the industrial dishwasher.

"Well, fuck me sideways. Did you get a gander at those three?"

Ivory didn't even jump at the voice or blink at the crass words as she continued to stack the dishwasher. "You are so articulate, Libby."

"Hey, you didn't hire me for my mouth," was the quick, sassy reply.

Libby Fontane was another employee – waitress and bartender extraordinaire – who never failed to get the best tips. She was classically beautiful with blonde hair, blue eyes, full lips, and an even fuller cleavage. And she also happened to be Ivory's best friend.

Hitting the big green button on the stainless steel appliance, she turned and ran a critical eye over the blonde bombshell. "Remind me – why did I hire you again?"

"Ha ha, you're hilarious. But seriously, who were they? Did you get their names? Where are they staying? Do you think they'll be back?"

Rolling her eyes, Ivory leaned against the counter, deciding it was easier to answer Libby's questions than it was to ignore them. Libby was rather tenacious. "I have no idea who they were, no – I didn't get their names, no clue where they're staying, and I highly doubt they'll be back. I'm sure they were just passing through."

That last statement brought a twinge of disappointment. She would have really liked to have seen them all again. Which was nuts, she assured herself. She had only laid eyes on them for a few minutes.

"Ivory!" Libby moaned. "Don't tell me you wasted a perfectly good opportunity to finally get some action. How long has it been since you got laid again? A year?"

She glared at her friend. "It has not been a year!" Eleven and a half months was not a year, she assured herself. "Besides, what opportunity? They hightailed it out of here quick-smart."

Libby's eyes widened in apparent disbelief. "You're kidding, right? Couldn't you feel the heat they were generating in your direction? Hell, I was across the room and I could feel it."

Ivory burst out laughing – she couldn't help it. Hers was not a face that generated heat. Especially not from three sex gods with broad shoulders and cotton tee shirts that stretched tightly across defined pectorals and biceps. She looked down at herself and saw faded black jeans, a plain black tee shirt, and serviceable black shoes. She gestured to herself. "I'm not sure how they held back with all of *this* standing in front of them."

"I'm serious, Ivory. My horny radar is foolproof. And those men were most definitely horny – for you. All of them, I might add." Libby's face was quite earnest – an unusual look for her.

Snorting, Ivory shook her head. "I really wish that was true, but because I live on planet Earth and not planet Orgasm, I'm thinking my celibacy is safe for a while yet."

"But—"

"Besides," she cut in, "what in the world would I do with three of them at once?"

Libby shook her head sadly as if Ivory was the biggest disappointment in the world. "Oh, honey. That may be the most depressing thing I have ever heard you say."

They stared at each other solemnly for a few seconds before breaking into a fit of giggles that would make fourth graders proud. She didn't really need a pack of men when she had friends like Libby. Although she had lied – she knew exactly what she would do if she had the three of them in her bed at once.

And there was nothing depressing about it.

Three

hree hours later, Ivory had successfully shut up shop with no further incidents. She'd had to consciously force her thoughts away from the three mystery men a number of times throughout the night. And although she was a little embarrassed by how infatuated she was with them, it had also been a welcome distraction, taking her mind off her troubles.

But as she neared the top of her stairs, her evening of reprieve was shattered. There, on her doorstep, was a small harmless-looking package wrapped in brown paper. She approached it with trepidation, now uneasy about entering her own home – her sanctuary – the one place she had fought for single-mindedly for years. It was something she resented immensely, and it pissed her off enough to have her stomping up the remaining two steps and snatching up the parcel.

Almost every night for the last week, there had been a 'gift' waiting for her on her doorstep or in the mail. The surprises had been coming for a while now, but lately they had been getting more frequent . . . and more disturbing. It had all started a few months ago – small things which seemed harmless at first. A bunch of flowers here, a box of chocolates there. At first, she had been quite taken by the gifts and her secret admirer. What girl didn't like a bit of intrigue and romance? But after a few weeks, when the gifts kept coming with no name or return address, she had begun to feel a little uneasy. A secret admirer was one thing, but some anonymous creeper was another.

When a dozen white roses had shown up at the bar with no note for the third time, she decided to bin the lot. Two days after she had thrown out the blooms, she woke up to a small, neatly wrapped package on her doorstep. Feeling more curious than anything else, she had immediately removed the brown paper and opened the box – only to fling it halfway across the room. The box was filled with decaying white rose petals and a note that read: 'Bad

Ivory.' To say it had freaked her out was an under-statement. She had no doubt her secret admirer discovered she'd disposed of his generous present, and he wasn't happy about it.

Libby had been outraged on her behalf when Ivory explained the ongoing situation. But she had also been worried and demanded Ivory go to the police immediately. But she was reluctant to get the police involved – a fact she couldn't explain to Libby or anyone else. Her current name, bank accounts, tax file number, and identification photos were only five years old. Although they were well done, she couldn't take the risk of them being found to be fraudulent. She loved it here – the bar was her dream and the three-bedroom apartment above it had taken her months of renovations to make it perfect. It was her home.

So, she'd laughed it off, keeping the numerous other strange happenings to herself until about two weeks ago, when she found a dead rabbit with a red bow tied around its neck in her letterbox. Dead flowers were one thing, but dead animals were another nightmare entirely. She confessed to Libby that her admirer had never really gone away. After much swearing, ranting, and tears, Libby suggested a bodyguard because it was clear Ivory had no intention of going to the police. Again, she'd hesitated – she didn't want anyone in her space. What if they discovered her secret? She wasn't exactly running from anything, but she was most definitely hiding. Some might consider it cowardice to hide – she didn't. She considered it smart. So, in the interest of being smart once again, she finally caved and called the bodyguard business Libby had researched and recommended. He was coming tomorrow.

Looking down at the brown package she held, she decided to leave it unopened until then. Let her bodyguard deal with it. That's what she was paying him for, after all. A quick check determined her front door remained secure – the matchstick she left in the doorjamb was still solidly in place. As far as security systems went, she knew it was a pretty shitty one. She had installed a state-of-the-art electronic one inside, but she still liked to see the physical proof that no-one had touched her door.

Unlocking the door and disarming the alarm quickly, she simply leaned her head back against the solid wood. What she wouldn't give to have three muscle-bound men keeping her company right now. Shaking her head over her wasted thoughts, she locked her deadbolt and secured her chain in place. She really wished she could have placed her own personal safety mechanisms around her apartment. Hell, she could probably even have searched out her creeper if she really tried. But then, that would expose her to the very people she was trying to hide from in the first place.

And it would expose her for what she truly was: a witch.

Four

The dawn broke cold and grey. *Just a little bit depressing,* Ronan thought as he stretched his limbs, cramped from the tiny hotel bed. His feet were hanging off the end of the bed and his neck was stiff as hell.

Cheap hotel beds were not made for men of their size and what made matters worse – he had drawn the short straw and had been forced into the single bed the evening before. Looking to his left, he saw that Seth and Vaughn were still nestled quite cosily together in the queen bed. Reminding himself he had been lucky enough to win the 'rock off' on their three previous jobs, he forced himself to stop pouting and get out of bed.

Ten minutes later, he had showered and shaved

and was dressed for the day to meet their new client. Stopping in the doorway of the bathroom, he noticed the other two were yet to make a move. *Lazy beasts*, he thought, but it was with affection rather than rancour. If they could have, Ronan knew they would both sleep in till noon. A soft purr he recognised as Vaughn's had him looking that way again. Vaughn was now awake, a rhythmic satisfied purr rumbling lazily in his chest as he stroked a calloused hand over Seth's back. Ronan smiled. Vaughn's biggest secret? He was a snuggler.

"Time to get up, boys," he said, walking to the small desk and taking his phone off the charger. Their new client was supposed to email them with their meet-up point today.

"Don't wanna . . ." came the muttered reply from Seth.

"What he said," Vaughn followed up, neither making a move.

Ronan rolled his eyes. They went through the same routine every morning. They'd start moving soon enough, probably because one of them would grab the other one's morning wood, but still . . . Scrolling through his phone, he saw they had an unopened email in their business inbox from more than an hour ago. Their new client was an early riser, apparently.

"Move it, fellas. We got our email," he threw over his shoulder, as he tapped on his phone screen to open it. Their client suggested they meet at nine, and the location . . . "Huh."

"Huh, what?" Seth asked, planting a kiss on the top of his head from behind.

"You're never going to believe the address for the meet with our mysterious client." He angled his phone so Seth could see it. A huge yawn and a creaking bed signalled Vaughn had also deigned to get up, and Ronan tapped at the address, bringing it to his attention as well.

"Hastings Lane? Why does that sound familiar?" Vaughn asked.

"Because it's the address of the bar we were at last night," Seth pointed out.

The bar with the sexy female proprietor, Ronan thought, without really knowing why. The woman was as plain as could be in the looks department. There was nothing particularly remarkable about her brown hair and eyes, and her body had been hidden behind practical clothes. But there was no denying he'd felt an instant spark of attraction to the woman the moment he laid eyes on her. He'd spent the better part of the night feeling guilty over his continued hardness – for the first time in years, it wasn't the result of the two men sleeping so close. The time for sharing their bed with others had long passed. So why was he finding himself so enamoured with some strange woman he'd met for all of two minutes? It didn't make sense.

It was also the reason why he had ushered them all out of the bar last night so quickly. He hadn't wanted to give away his thoughts by remaining in her presence any longer. Although, he had his suspicions regarding his partners anyway. He could have sworn he had seen lust shining in Seth's eyes the evening before, as well as suppressed desire in Vaughn's. None of them said anything about it before going to bed, and although they engaged in their usual nightly play, he couldn't help feeling like they had all been holding back a little.

"It's suspicious," Vaughn stated, posture going on alert.

Seth patted him on the back, heading into the bathroom. "It's a coincidence," he corrected.

Vaughn just grunted, scowling at the address on the phone screen. "Coincidences are fucking suspicious."

"You think everything is fucking something or

other," Seth retorted, his voice garbled from the toothbrush hanging from the corner of his mouth.

"And I'm always right," Vaughn shouted back, and Seth merely flipped him off as he moved to rinse his mouth. "Well I am, aren't I?" his grumpy lover demanded.

Ronan shook his head. The two men were always bickering about something. Not that it concerned him. After all, it was all foreplay. "I'm not enabling you two."

It had been a big adjustment, not only for them but for their panthers, when Seth showed up ten years ago. His arrival challenged them in every way possible. For starters, his panther was a big dominant bastard, and he knew Vaughn's cat initially struggled with having another alpha in their shadow – what they called their little feline group. In the wild, male black jaguars were not known for forming social groups, and they would usually carve out a large territory for themselves. They would only come together to mate and breed with a female. Male panthers were pretty much all alphas – making a group hierarchy a little redundant. It had never been a problem for Vaughn or himself over the generations because his own beast had no desire to challenge Vaughn's in any way. Seth's, on the other hand, was all about pushing boundaries – the biggest being their feelings for each other. And that was something Ronan would be forever grateful for.

He had been harbouring feelings for Vaughn pretty much since their first incarnation. At that time, it was easy enough to ignore his desires. Their coven was thriving and complete with twelve members, and they were familiars to their own individual witches. Over the generations, the Panthera Coven's numbers dwindled – along with the familiars – and they found themselves thrown together more and more. His attraction grew with every generation, but he never acted on it for a multitude of reasons. The biggest reason being that their lives were not their own. Hell, even their deaths weren't their exclusive property, given they were reborn again and again. They were bound to serve their coven and their bloodlines for eternity. As far as he was aware, no familiar had ever had their own family before.

Two generations ago, there had just been him, Vaughn, and one other female familiar left in their coven, and a solo male witch named Dale. They shared the responsibilities, and with their panthers already being so accustomed to each other, had settled into a surprisingly easy truce. When Dale was killed in an accident at the age of twenty-one along-side Maree, his female familiar, he never even had the chance to make his own family, thus effectively wiping out the Panthera bloodline – or so they assumed.

Vaughn had spiralled into a rather nasty depression and Ronan managed to keep himself from his own pit of despair only because the other man needed him. With no witch left in their coven, their whole purpose for being was over. Not only would they never be reborn again, but they were also outcasts in the witching world. What use was a familiar without a witch? Time seemed to crawl by in that last life – endless days and nights with no future. His only solace was Vaughn, despite the man's hard exterior and shitty attitude. Ronan believed it had literally broken his heart when Vaughn died in his sleep at age eighty-three, for he died not a month later. The real surprise came when they were both born again, finding and recognising each other in their early teens. Unbelievable as it was, the only explanation was that there was another member of their coven out there somewhere. Some-how, someway, there was a surviving witch.

Vaughn refused to believe it at first, arguing with him constantly. But then, a little over ten years ago,

Ronan walked into a bar to peel Vaughn from yet another fight, when his panther scented another predator in the room. Seth was the man Vaughn had been pummelling – or attempting to, anyway. Seth held his own, even at twenty years of age. After a lot of swearing, arguing, and discussions, they had finally determined Seth was indeed a familiar. And not only a familiar, but a black jaguar, a panther – just like them. It shouldn't have been possible. Only familiars charged with serving the Panthera Coven shared their spirits with the panther, and their bloodline was extinct. But with the appearance of Seth came further proof that a witch must be out there somewhere.

After those initial arguments and the adjustment to the dominant nature of Seth's cat, Seth started to challenge them in new ways. He was a happy-go-lucky, easy-going man, but he was also damn stubborn and chased after what he wanted with a single-minded purpose. And it soon became clear that he wanted the both of them. Ronan shook his head in remembrance; the pure shock on Vaughn's face when Seth told them to make out in front of him because he was in the mood for live porn was priceless. Ronan would forever be grateful for the younger miscreant because he couldn't remember ever being happier in all his lives as he was right now. Although he didn't have his coven or his witch, he had the love of two men, and he would be quite happy to live out the rest of his days in his little shadow of three.

"Earth to Ronan." Snapping fingers in front of his face brought him back to the present. "Dude, where were you?" Seth asked.

"I was—"

"Never mind where his damn head was at. We need to discuss this case." Vaughn snatched the phone out of his hand, scrolling through the saved emails from their client.

Ronan sighed. Had he really just thought how perfectly in love he was with the big oaf? "Way to ruin the moment," he muttered.

"What moment?" The question came from Seth, who was now fully dressed and shaved.

He sighed, reaching up and running his fingers through the silky softness of Seth's onyx hair. "A sentimental moment. He ruined it and now you're my favourite," he jested, tugging playfully on the inky strands.

"The kid's always your favourite," was Vaughn's somewhat absent response, but there was no animosity in it. None of them were insecure and none of them played favourites.

Seth grinned. "I'm your favourite too. Admit it, you love me being in the middle."

Vaughn deigned to flick his eyes up at that, and the heat in them was plain to see. Oh, yes, they loved it when Seth was in the middle.

"Enough playtime. We need to discuss this meet. We don't know anything about this job. The client was suspiciously obtuse in their emails," Vaughn grumbled.

Ronan chose to ignore Seth's snicker over Vaughn's use of the word *suspicious* again. What Vaughn said was actually true. They had received an email just days ago from an unknown female asking for help regarding a stalker. She hadn't volunteered any details about her apparent stalker, nor had she volunteered her name. She had merely outlined her situation in vague terms and agreed to pay their fee if they were able to get here within the week. There weren't many enemies left for their kind, but true witch hunters still existed, and every familiar was on constant watch for signs of their presence. However, their numbers had dwindled considerably over the years. Still, he wouldn't put it past them to set a trap for their shadow – witch hunters didn't discriminate between killing witches and familiars. A magical being was a magical being to them, and they hunted them all with equal fervour.

"We'll tread carefully," he told the others. "And if it turns out to be more than a simple job, we'll inform the marshals and the conclave."

They were still on good speaking terms with the conclave – the witching governing body – despite the fact they were deemed useless regarding their roles as familiars. The marshals also came in handy every so often. They were essentially the police within the witch society, and they had often worked with the marshals in the past when the conclave had ordered it.

"I wouldn't mind at all if it turns out to be hunters," Vaughn stated brazenly. "I could use a good fight."

And therein lies his problem, Ronan mused. Vaughn could *always* use a good fight. Ronan just hoped the mysterious owner of the bar wasn't involved with the hunters in any way. The thought of harming her made him a little sick to his stomach.

Five

The sick feeling in Ronan's stomach morphed quickly into butterflies when the woman from the night before unlocked the door to the closed bar and gestured them inside after checking their identifications. It seemed his inexplicable attraction from the previous evening hadn't been a one-off. *Damn.*

"Please, come in. I have to admit, I wasn't expecting to see you all again. You're really from Sentry Bodyguard Services?" She sounded disbelieving . . . and just a touch suspicious. Ronan didn't blame her.

"You saw our identification," Vaughn declared, his voice gruff and his statement sharp, even for him. Did he feel the connection too? Was that why he was acting defensively?

The woman cleared her throat. "Yes, well. My apologies for last night. I'm sure Trucker Pete said something entirely inappropriate."

"Trucker Pete?" Seth raised his brows as he eyed her up and down.

She laughed, the throaty sound going straight to Ronan's dick. "That's what I call him. Pete's a regular."

Vaughn snorted. "A regular arsehole maybe."

Her grin widened at that. "You're not wrong. But he's also fairly harmless – when he's sober, that is. Anyway, I'm Ivory. I suppose we should get down to business . . .?" she trailed off, looking around the bar as if it would somehow ease the awkwardness in the room.

It was clear she was tense and nervous, and his panther could also smell the acrid scent of fear. The aroma bothered him on a primal level and had his animal wanting to rub up against her in comfort. Instead, he put on his professional hat and gestured to a table. "Maybe we could sit, and you could tell us what's been going on."

Ivory nodded, straightening her shoulders. "Yes, of course. Please sit. Ronan, right?" Her gaze flicked to him as they made their way to a six-seater table.

Firmly ignoring the thrill he got from hearing his name on her lips, he dipped his head in acknowledgement. "Right. And this is Seth and Vaughn." He gestured to his companions, reconfirming the names she had seen on their identifications.

She glanced at each of them in turn before speaking further. "Thank you for coming. I've been having some . . . issues lately."

Seth leaned forwards on the chair he was straddling. It wasn't very professional of him, but it was a habit Ronan hadn't been able to break him of yet. "What kind of issues?"

"Creeper issues."

"Creeper issues?" Seth wasn't winning any eloquence awards today.

Ivory nodded. "Uh huh. At first, I just thought I had a secret admirer, you know? I received flowers, chocolates . . . things like that. No card, no return address. The first month or so, they were all rather innocuous . . ."

"But then they stopped being innocent?" Seth prompted.

She laughed a little. "You could say that. Photos, underwear, and last week . . . a dead rabbit."

That got Vaughn's attention, and he sat up straighter. "A dead animal?"

She swallowed hard, looking a little green. "Yes. It was in my letterbox. I think it had been drowned."

The three of them glanced at each other; that wasn't good. If the stalker was escalating to that degree, he or she was becoming unstable. "Have you kept everything from this stalker? The letters, the gifts?" Vaughn asked.

"Not at the beginning, no. But after the first few weeks, I did."

"Good. Why don't you go grab it all for us so we can see what we're working with? Then we can go from there," he suggested.

Ivory released a pent-up breath and nodded her head. She stood without further comment, practically running from the room. The movement disrupted the air and caused her scent to waft over Ronan once again. He breathed deep – it was delicious . . . and oddly familiar.

"Well? What do we think?" Ronan asked, leaving unspoken that he was questioning the legitimacy of the job. They would know what he was alluding to.

"She's scared. I'll give her that," Vaughn acknowledged.

Seth nodded. "She definitely is. And I didn't scent

any deceit. I think we can rule out her being a hunter, but there's just something about her . . . I can't put my finger on it," he muttered, looking in the direction Ivory had disappeared.

"I can," Ronan asserted. The knowledge had just slammed into him moments before. "She smells like us – like all of us." *And it's driving me insane,* he added to himself.

The other two looked surprised, taking deep breaths and trying to capture the lingering scent of the female who had just left.

Vaughn grunted. "You're right. She smells like rain, earth, and vanilla." He turned and faced Ronan. "You always smell like fresh green grass to me, or falling leaves in autumn. Fresh, crisp . . . welcoming."

Ronan thought for a moment. "And you always smell like an approaching storm – wild and turbulent, fresh and powerful."

Seth was nodding but frowning at the same time. "I agree. But she also smells like vanilla." He scrunched his nose up. "I don't smell like vanilla."

Ronan winced internally. Something told him Seth wasn't going to like hearing that he did, in fact, smell remarkably like the flavoured orchid. He turned to Vaughn. "You wanna tell him?"

"Tell me what?!" Seth already had a belligerent

look on his face and Ronan fought the chuckle building in his chest. He sure was cute when he was disgruntled.

Vaughn nodded, actually grinning for once – too bad it was at Seth's expense. "You, my little kitten, absolutely smell like vanilla. All sweet and tasty-like."

Seth gasped in outrage, looking positively horrified. "I do not!"

"You do," Ronan confirmed, but was very quick to add, "but it's not a bad thing. My cat loves it. He always wants to roll around in your scent."

His younger lover didn't seem convinced if his glower was anything to go by. "I do *not* smell like vanilla. I smell like dirt and sweat and all things manly," he grumbled.

Vaughn laughed, clearly enjoying Seth's discomfort as he draped an arm over his shoulders. "Hey now, it's not like we can all smell like thunder and lightning."

A sharp jab to Vaughn's ribs only caused his arm to tighten as he brushed his head against Seth's shoulder. Ronan heard a deep inhale and then a rumbling purr that served to stir up his own inner panther. "Don't fight it, kitten. You smell sexy . . ." His tongue darted out to lick a long line up Seth's neck, before nibbling on the exposed flesh behind his ear. "... You *taste* sexy."

A squeak from behind them had him spinning to find Ivory standing in the doorway. Her eyes darted between them, lingering on Vaughn and Seth before she cleared her throat, looking pointedly away. Ronan frowned at her obvious discomfort. Did she have a problem with men being together? He was surprised how disappointed he was in her. Wondering why her opinions should matter to him so much on such short acquaintance, he almost missed Vaughn's deep breath in. The satisfied purr that followed wasn't loud enough to be perceived by human ears, but his panther heard it loud and clear.

What the hell? he wondered, shocked by Vaughn's reaction. But then he smelt it: arousal, sharp and ripe, permeating the air. And it was distinctly feminine. Out of all of them, Vaughn had the best sense of smell and had obviously picked up the scent before he or Seth.

Well, well, well, Ronan thought. Seemed his initial assumption about Ivory's reaction had been wrong. Now, wasn't that interesting?

Six

I vory took a deep breath, attempting to gain control of her rapidly beating heart. When she had entered, the two largest of the men had been wrapped around each other and it was all she could do not to lick her lips. Talk about a turn-on. She'd never really thought of herself as particularly kinky before and although she enjoyed the odd daydream about being pleasured by a harem of hot men, she had never entertained the possibility in real life. Well, she sure as shit was now!

Vaughn had his arm wrapped around Seth and the bigger man had been leaning into him, clearly trusting in his lover's strength to keep them both upright. Vaughn's mouth had been at Seth's neck and all she could think of was how she wanted to be in the middle of it all. Strong, masculine arms surrounding her, hard bodies pressing in from all sides as lips and tongues explored at their leisure . . . *Sigh* . . .

Quickly averting her eyes before any of the men noticed the lust lasering from them, she caught a glimpse of herself in the mirror on the wall . . . and sighed all over again. But this time, it was in resignation. She patted her hair self-consciously, hating the mousey-brown colour and the limp look of it. Her dull brown eyes, rounded freckled face, and nondescript clothes completed her appearance, and she found herself cursing the magical glamour for the first time in years.

Never being a vain person, she hadn't really been too concerned with the necessity of the glamour – she altered her appearance to save her life. Full stop. She'd rather be alive and safe than preening in the mirror every morning. But right now, faced with the trio of male perfection in front of her, she wished she could reveal her true features. Her bright-purple eyes and snow-white hair were always eye-catching – and that was exactly why she had been forced to use a glamour in the first place. Her countenance was too striking, too unusual – even the humans unaware of magic wouldn't fail to notice her other-worldly appearance.

Her self-pity was for naught anyway, she chided herself. Seth and Vaughn were clearly in a relation-ship, which meant she had the wrong equipment to bring to the party. *Stupid breasts,* she berated, scowling at them accusingly.

"Ivory? Everything okay?"

The deep voice had her jerking from her ridicu-lous inner ramblings. *Focus, Ivory. Focus!* "Yes. Sorry. I, ah, I have everything you asked for." She held up the box containing all the notes and 'gifts' her creepy stalker had given her.

She walked back over to them a little cautiously. What were the chances the same three men of her dreams from the night before would be the same men from the security company she had contacted the week prior? It was a strange coincidence, but at the same time, their little town didn't have a whole lot of watering holes. The chance of them walking into hers was relatively high . . . she supposed. Boy, she really hoped she wasn't making excuses for them because they happened to be pretty. She wished she could whip up a spell and peek into their heads –

and other naughtier places. Unfortunately, her glamour prevented it. Yes, it altered her appearance and hid her magical energy from other magic users, but it also worked the other way as well – dampening her powers, her senses, and even inhibiting her natural instincts. Three things she really could have used right now.

She placed the large box on the table, pushing it into the middle so they could all see its contents. The men stood in order to peer inside more fully, and Ivory was blessed with the chance to appreciate the obvious strength in their bodies and the height of their frames. She had been right last night; they were well over six feet, with Seth being about two inches taller than Vaughn and three inches taller than Ronan. Seth was also carrying the most muscle – a fact she found intriguing given he was clearly the youngest.

She put him at around her age of thirty, if not a little younger. Ronan looked to be mid-thirties, while Vaughn was perhaps late-thirties or a very good-looking forty. She wondered if Seth was like a boy toy for the older man, but then remembered the way Vaughn had been looking at Seth when he had his arm wrapped around him. There was definite heat there, but also warmth. No, she decided, the relationship must be emotional as well as physical. She tried really hard not to let the green-eyed monster rear its ugly head over that. Jealousy was a very unattractive trait.

"What's this?" Seth asked, pointing to the unwrapped parcel from the night before.

That's right. There was a box full of disturbing trinkets from a likely psychopath in front of her. She'd do well to focus on that rather than the three men rummaging around in it. "It was on my doorstep last night after I closed down the bar. I decided not to open it because I knew I was meeting with you first thing this morning." She glared at the newest package, resenting its existence. She hardly slept at all last night because she'd been so tempted to open it and see what was inside. It was like some kind of sick, morbid curiosity. She knew it wouldn't be anything good, yet she couldn't help wanting to rip the paper open. Even now, with the three men eyeing the innocent-looking brown paper, she wanted to yell at them to get into it.

"What time did you discover it last night?" Ronan asked.

"Just after three in the morning. The bar closes at

three, so it was maybe twenty minutes after that," she answered.

"Do you always close the bar at that time?" The question came from Seth.

"No. I mean, yes – the bar closes at three. But I'm not always the person who works the late shift. I'm on rotation with two other staff."

"Is it the same rotation every week?" he followed up.

She shook her head, chewing on her bottom lip. Apparently, they weren't just the hired muscle but also had some brain power behind them too. "It's supposed to be," she offered, in answer to Seth's second question. "But I'm really flexible with the staff. Last-minute changes to work hours happen almost every week."

Vaughn grunted at that. "You're going to have to tell us your routines: what time you get up, what time you go to work, when you go to the grocery store, when you break for meals. And everything else in every minute of your day."

Every minute of the day? She forced herself not to fuss nervously with her hair or chew on her fingernails. This protection thing was going to be far more invasive than she had counted on. How she going to keep her past a secret? She really didn't like to lie. And yes, she knew how hypocritical that was given her entire face was one big illusion.

Ronan must have picked up on her nerves, for he encouraged, "I know it sounds like we're being nosy, but not only will that information help keep you safe, it will allow us to piece together a timeline of when your stalker has made contact in the past. Hopefully, we'll be able to determine his routine and have him caught in no time."

She nodded her head, appreciating his logic. But it didn't make her any less nervous. "The package . . ." she prompted, distracting herself and them from her anxiety.

Seth looked towards the other two and Ronan gave a slight nod of his head. Clearly, that was all the go-ahead Seth needed, for he whipped out a switchblade from his pocket and proceeded to slip the knife edge under the tape holding the paper in place. A few deft slices and the paper fell away to reveal a plain white box.

"Look familiar?" he asked.

She was already nodding her head. "All the packages have been wrapped identically: brown paper, white box. All the notes are the same too: white envelopes, plain paper, black pen."

"Well, let's see what we have in here, shall we?"

Seth used the tip of the blade to push the lid of the box back.

Black lace was folded neatly inside and he prodded it around just enough for her to make out that it was a g-string. *Lovely,* she thought, *more lingerie.* It had become a favourite present from her admirer over the past few weeks. She actually loved indulging in exotic lingerie and had a rather extensive collection in the top drawer of her dresser. She had to fight against the negative association every time she slipped into something satin or silk these days. But she wasn't going to let the bastard take away her joy over her pretties.

The men were still staring at the black lacey piece of underwear and she wondered what was holding their attention for so long. She looked a little closer and almost gagged; there was a distinctive off-white, crusty substance covering a large part of the material. "Tell me that isn't what I think it is." She clapped a hand over her mouth, already knowing the answer, but Vaughn spoke anyway.

"If you think it's jizz, then you are absolutely correct."

"Vaughn!" Ronan's voice was reproachful over the seemingly blasé comment. But one look at Vaughn's face, and Ivory knew he was far from amused. His light-green eyes were cold and hard, his jaw clenched so tightly she feared his teeth would crack.

For some reason, his insult and anger on her behalf made her feel better, and she relaxed a little. "Gross," she muttered, screwing her face up in disgust and turning away.

Ronan pushed the lid back onto the box, blocking the foul sight from view. "Has this happened before? Have you ever received anything sexual? Anything with evidence of his release?"

She sat back down and gestured to the large box in the middle of the table. "Some lingerie, massage oil, chocolate body paint. But nothing with" – she arched a brow in Vaughn's direction – "jizz on it."

Vaughn's lips twitched, and he dipped his head in her direction, before pulling the items out of the box. "Will you put these in chronological order for us, please?"

She spent the next hour explaining the origins of the items and the timeframe. The men asked numerous questions – many she had already thought of, but some she hadn't. Maybe Libby had been right when she recommended bodyguards. She was feeling safer already – from her stalker, at least. She was still feeling very insecure regarding keeping her secrets hidden and also over the general hotness of the guys. Both could prove to be dangerous distractions.

Finally, Vaughn leaned back in his chair with a huge sigh. "Well, I'd say you've got yourself a predatory stalker."

"So you don't think I'm overreacting?" she held her breath in anticipation of their answer. She didn't know whether she wanted them to tell her she was being a drama queen or that her fears were valid.

"No, we don't," Ronan assured her. "There are multiple typologies that can be used to help categorise a stalker's behaviour. As Vaughn said, your description of the events and the evidence in this box here are very reminiscent of a predatory stalker. Although, it's interesting – it looks like it started out more intimacy-seeking and has now devolved."

"I take it that's a bad thing," she guessed.

Seth was frowning even as he nodded. "Unfortunately, yes. You see, these very early notes and gifts – they were innocent, romantic even, as if he were trying to entice you into a real relationship. Over time, the correspondence became bitter, then angry, but now it is filled with rage. The dead rabbit is another example of that rage. Usually, intimacy-seeking stalkers believe their victim is their one true love and that their love is reciprocated. I imagine not returning his love letters and throwing out his precious gifts made him think you did not, in fact, love him back."

"Of course I don't love him!" she exclaimed. "I don't even know him!"

"That's not what he believes. And it's likely not all that accurate either. The vast majority of stalkers are friends or family. At the very least, acquaintances. Chances are, you've met him."

Even though she had considered that possibility, had even scrutinised all her staff and customers, it still gave her a serious case of the heebie-jeebies. She shook it off, knowing they would soon be investigating everyone she knew anyway. "You said predatory stalker. Sounds ominous."

"It is," Vaughn growled. "Predatory stalkers aren't interested in a relationship. Their focus is on control, violence, and sexual gratification. They're total nut jobs," Vaughn added, in what she was beginning to realise was his typical blunt way.

"Great." She blew out a breath, pushing her loosened hair back. "So . . . what now?"

"Now we check out your bar, your apartment – any of your frequent haunts. We need to analyse your current level of security and also see where we'll be staying."

"What? Staying?" She sat up straight. "You're going to stay here? All of you?" Man, she really hoped her voice didn't sound so breathless to their ears because it sure did to her own.

Vaughn frowned – actually, it was closer to a glower, and Ivory was beginning to understand it was a common expression for him. She wished it was a turn-off. She really didn't enjoy sullen men. But she found the way the lines crinkled around his eyes sexy. And the way his nose scrunched up just a little with every scowl? Totally adorable! She shook her head. She was losing it. Maybe Libby was right, her last sexcapades had been far too long ago and now she was suffering from too much estrogen or something. An outlet. She needed an outlet, that was all.

"Of course we'll be staying here. That's what you hired us for, isn't it? A personal bodyguard?" Vaughn followed up his sexy, adorable glare with his sexy, adorable voice.

Yep. Definitely losing it. She had to think of something fast. Not only did she not want strangers in her space – what if they found her witchy stash? She also did not trust herself around them. She totally did not want these three men to become her outlet – no matter what her hormones thought. "No. I mean yes. Yes, I did hire a personal bodyguard. But I thought there was just one of you. I mean, how much is this going to cost me? I can't afford your fee times three."

There, she congratulated herself, *that sounded logical.*

"The fee we quoted you is for all of us. We work as a team." Vaughn's response was flat, no nonsense.

"Ivory . . ." Ronan's deep voice drew her attention, ". . . you have a stalker. One who has been sending you things for months, including soiled underwear and dead animals right to your doorstep. He knows where you live, Ivory. Let us help you. This is what we do."

And with that happy reminder, Ivory's lust extinguished. They were right. There was some crazy person out there going around killing bunnies in order to gain her attention. All the years hiding, uprooting herself from town to town . . . she was sick of it. She loved it here. She wouldn't be forced out of her home by some whack-job. She just had to be careful what she said and did in front of her bodyguards. She had no doubt they were good at their jobs. The barest whiff that she was hiding something, and she was positive they would sniff out every single one of her secrets. And if that happened, having a stalker wouldn't matter anyway – she would have to run again. But ultimately, she needed help, and she needed it now.

"You're right. I'm sorry. This is just a little over-whelming for me. I still find it hard to believe anyone would go to so much trouble over this." She flapped a hand at herself.

Ronan scoffed. "What do you mean? You're beau-tiful. I'm sure you have men lining up."

Ivory looked at him in shock. He thought she was beautiful? That was not going to help her aforemen-tioned estrogen problem. He seemed just as stunned by his admission as she was, if the horrified expres-sion on his face was anything to go by. Looking around, she saw Vaughn's infamous scowl firmly in place and what appeared to be a knowing – and very amused – smirk on Seth's lips.

Ronan cleared his throat. "Anyway, let's get to it. Seth, you check the perimeter. Vaughn, scope out Ivory's apartment. I'll go grab our stuff from the hotel and check out. I'll meet you back here in about an hour," he finished, standing to his impressive height.

Vaughn stopped him before he could make it

three steps. "Be careful," he demanded. "Guys like this tend to be voyeurs. Chances are he won't take kindly to three men making house with the object of his desire."

"Yes, dear," was Ronan's response, and Vaughn proceeded to—

Ivory's mouth fell open for the second time that morning. Vaughn had just growled sexily and then kissed Ronan full on the mouth.

What the . . .? She must have made some sound – hopefully not some kind of weird mating call like she wanted to – for Vaughn narrowed his eyes.

"Yes?" He fired the word at her.

"Nothing! It's just that . . . well, I thought you two were a couple. I mean, you and Seth . . ." She stammered. *Smooth, real smooth, Ivory.*

"We are," Vaughn crossed his arms a little belligerently. "But so are Ronan and I, and Seth and Ronan. We're all in a relationship."

"Oh," was the only response her dry mouth could muster. They were *all* in a relationship.

"Do you have a problem with that?" Ronan asked, moss-green eyes narrowed in her direction.

Hell yes, she had a problem with that. She had a problem because she wanted to tackle the three of them to the floor and get to the sweaty, messy, satisfying, kinky sex this instant! The three of them were together? All of them? At the same time? It was like a dream come true, an honest to goodness fantasy brought to life.

Instead of saying all that out loud though, she merely squeaked, "No. No problem."

Seven

Vaughn studied their newest client with great interest. He was wildly attracted to her – since the moment he had first heard that throaty voice of hers. Ignoring the very peculiar fact that she smelled like a mixture of all of them, he had no idea why such chemistry would be there. She wasn't anything like his previous type in women.

He had liked them tall, stacked, and dumb. It was superficial and shallow of him, but that's exactly what he had been before his relationship with Ronan and Seth. He had definitely been the love 'em and leave 'em type. He couldn't even blame it on the fact that familiars rarely indulged in long-term relationships. He simply had no desire to commit to anyone – ever – despite the warm, fuzzy feelings and rampant desire he'd suppressed for Ronan throughout the generations.

Until Seth barged into their lives, Vaughn had honestly never contemplated acting on those desires. But the kid made a compelling argument, and he had never looked back. So why was he practically hypnotised by the sway of Ivory's feminine hips as she preceded him up the stairs? It was very curious. And despite the old adage, 'curiosity killed the cat,' he fully intended to indulge his curiosity.

"How long have you lived here?" he asked, taking the key from her hands before she could slide it into the lock. "Let me go in first."

She pressed her lips together tightly but didn't say anything, allowing him to insert the key and open the door. "Almost five years now," she answered, as he stepped into the room, his heightened hearing confirming the apartment was indeed empty.

"Did you always want to be a bar owner?" he questioned, trying to get a feel for her as their client, but also genuinely interested in getting to know her better. She didn't really have the look of a bar owner – wasn't edgy enough.

The room he stepped into didn't mesh with what he knew of the woman standing next to him, either.

It was filled with bold colours, oversized furniture and a truly eclectic array of art. A huge built-in bookcase graced an entire wall, and teal lounges with striped cushions sectioned off the living area from the open-plan kitchen with its white quartz counter tops and dark-stained cabinets. The huge rug dominating the whitewashed floors was a striking magenta with the remaining furniture all dark wood and antique looking.

"Problem?" she asked, peering around him.

He must have been staring longer than he thought. "No. Your apartment . . ."

"What about it?" She crossed her arms over her chest, plumping up breasts that looked to be a convenient handful.

"It's interesting – homey," he added, seeing her frown. And it was. The whole space may have looked like a rainbow vomited everywhere, but it somehow worked with the colours complimenting each other, even though they should have contrasted.

She eyed him suspiciously for a moment before nodding her head. "It is homey – *my* home. I worked hard to create this space. You should have seen the state it was in when I bought it. I did all the renovations and decorating myself." She smiled proudly.

"Yeah?" He was surprised. Most chicks weren't really into drywall and plumbing.

"Don't get too many ideas. I had help, I assure you. But it was fun and well worth the effort."

"Bedrooms?" he queried, stepping further into the room.

"Three. Down the hall that way. As well as a master bathroom and another odd little room that's too open to be a bedroom but too small to be another living area. I turned it into my study," she explained.

He merely grunted, walking down the wide hallway and checking out each room for security and just plain nosiness. The spare bedrooms were roomy, and both had decent queen-sized beds, although there was no way he and his two men would fit in one. Looked like they were back to the rock, paper, scissors to see who would be sleeping alone. The bathroom was likewise large, with an antique claw-foot tub and a big glassed-in shower. The windows in every room only had generic locks, so they were going to have to change those when they wired the windows up for . . .

His thoughts derailed when he came to Ivory's bedroom. If he thought the other rooms in the house were bold and surprising, then what could he call this one? Every wall was painted pitch black, and all the furnishings were white, including the wooden dresser and ornate chaise sofa under the large floor-to-ceiling window. The splashes of colour came in the form of a red shaggy rug, a huge painting of a brightly patterned sugar skull above her bed, and a yellow striped toy zebra that took up residence in the corner. But what really caught his attention was the bed; it was round. Ivory's bed was fucking round! It was also huge, considering the diminutive size of the woman. Hell, he figured he, Ronan, and Seth could fit on it with room to spare. Even their specially made king-sized bed at their house wasn't this big.

"Vaughn?"

Ivory's husky voice had him jolting in shock. Since when did he allow anyone to sneak up on him unawares? *When you start fantasising about your client naked in the middle of a round bed with your two long-term lovers,* he answered himself.

"You have a round bed," he uttered excitedly and without thought, before cursing himself when her eyebrows raised. He needed to get a grip here. She had hired them to do a job, and he was already falling down on it because of some misguided chemistry.

"Yes, I do," she responded slowly, looking at him as if he weren't all there.

Trying to recover from his rather inane comment, he went into full bodyguard mode. "Well, your security is pretty shit. That alarm system you installed is the cheapest one on the market and your window locks are pathetic."

He saw her lips firm and her jaw clench as if she were holding back her words. It didn't do much good because when she opened her mouth, all that came out was sarcasm. "My apologies. If I'd have known I was going to be stalked, I would have called the CIA and asked for their recommendation on window locks. And that alarm cost me four hundred dollars!"

His panther purred inside his head. The stupid animal loved to spar, and Ivory was giving as good as she was taking. "Thank you for acknowledging your shortcomings. In addition to updated security, from now on, you don't go anywhere alone. One of us will be with you everywhere you go, whether it's down in the bar or up here in your apartment."

Her brown eyes looked hot enough to incinerate him where he stood. "Don't you think that's a little excessive?"

He shrugged. "Fine, then. You're not interested in

the way we do things? We'll leave. Get yourself another bodyguard."

"Boy, you really are a hard-arse. Not really a social animal are you, Vaughn?"

If she only knew exactly what kind of animal he really was. "No, Ivory. I'm not. But you didn't hire me to be your BFF. We can help you – we really can. But if you're not willing to listen to us, this will never work."

"I'm not trying to be difficult – unlike someone else," She added, tossing an imperious look his way.

He smiled widely for the first time since meeting her – the lady sure had some spine. "It's best if you see the real me from the outset. That way, you can't say you weren't warned when you discover I'm not house-trained."

Wait, was that a joke? Did I really just make a joke? He was definitely losing his edge here.

She smiled, even chuckled a little. "I bet you leave the toilet seat up, huh?"

She managed to startle a laugh out of him. "I live with two other guys – the toilet seat always stays up." He saw her eyes dim a little with the reminder of his relationship status, but he didn't think it was because she disapproved. "Anyway," he began, rocking back on his heels a little, "who's your contact at the police department? What did they have to say about all of this?"

She hesitated and shifted restlessly from foot to foot. "Not much."

"Not much? That's not very informative. I'm going to need a copy of all the police reports – see how far into the investigation they are," Vaughn informed her. With any luck, the Po Po had already done half their work for them. They weren't private investigators by any stretch of the imagination, but sometimes they found themselves playing amateur detectives. He had a feeling this was going to be one of those times.

Ivory winced, muttering, "That's going to be a problem."

"And why is that?" He folded his arms over his chest, awaiting her slow response.

She sighed. "Because there are no police reports. And the reason the police haven't had much to say is because I haven't reported anything to them."

That was certainly interesting. She would have no reason not to involve the police unless she had something to hide. Despite the surprising reaction his dick had around the woman, he hadn't forgotten his reservations about the coincidental nature of the case. Not to mention the bizarre fact that she smelled like them all. He didn't necessarily think her unique scent was connected to why she was being stalked, but it was another strange piece to the mysterious puzzle that was their newest client.

"Why haven't you gone to the police?" he demanded.

She shrugged negligently. "Because I hired you instead."

"Try again, sweetheart. These threatening messages began months ago. Any average, single woman living alone would have been on the phone to the authorities in a heartbeat, crying her eyes out and pleading for help."

"Well, I'm not your average woman, am I?" she answered, her tone turning snotty.

She certainly wasn't. He was pushing her deliberately, trying to judge her reactions and also to see if she would slip up and reveal her secrets. However, their continued banter was having a different effect on him – in the crotch area. The spark of defiance and the sass in her vocabulary was making him hard, and he fought the urge to readjust himself.

He leaned closer, using his height to intimidate, and backed her up three steps until she was against the hallway wall. "What are you hiding, Ivory?"

Her head tilted back and the annoyed heat in her

eyes would have flayed a lesser man, he was sure. "None of your business."

"But you admit you are hiding something," he pointed out, surprised. He hadn't been expecting her to disclose that.

She shrugged, doing her best to appear uncaring when she really wasn't. Vaughn could hear her heart, and it was beating far faster than normal. "Sure, I admit it. But I'm entitled to my privacy. As long as it has no bearing on my current situation, I don't see how it's your business."

"How do you know it has nothing to do with the case? It could be directly related to your stalker. But we can't determine that until you tell us," he flung back. He leaned in closer, his body a bare inch from hers, and her pupils dilated as her nostrils flared. That was the exact same reaction Ronan had when he was aroused.

"You're just going to have to trust me the same way I'm going to have to trust you."

Her words were whispered, the warmth of her breath sighing against his lips. *Definitely aroused,* he decided.

Before he could make up his mind on what to do next, Ivory moved fast, ducking under his outstretched arm and clearing her throat. "If you'll excuse me, I have some accounts to go over. The bar opens in less than an hour, but I took the liberty of taking the day off today. I assumed we'd need time to go over things, plan a course of action. But I have employees that need to be paid, so I'll be spending some time working from my computer. Make yourself at home," she added, spinning on her heel and striding away briskly in the direction of her study.

He took the moment of privacy to bang his head soundly against the wall. She was going to be trouble. He could feel it.

Eight

A knock on the door forced Vaughn from his head bashing. Ivory had escaped to her study twenty minutes ago, and he had been staring after her ever since. Shaking himself from his stupor, he unlocked the door to find Ronan and Seth on the other side, loaded down with their luggage and equipment.

"Ivory?" Ronan questioned, dumping their stuff in the centre of the room.

"In her study," he replied. "Don't worry, I checked it out. It's relatively secure, but we're going to want to go over this place in more detail, set up our own system, change some locks . . ."

Ronan nodded, looking around the living space

83

with blatant curiosity. "This is nice. Really nice. Very much like the bar downstairs – unexpected."

He snorted sardonically. "Wait until you get a gander at her bedroom. Doesn't really match our dowdy client, does it?"

"She's not dowdy," Seth defended.

She wasn't dowdy at all. If she had been, Vaughn wouldn't have looked at her twice, let alone maintained continued interest in her.

He decided to placate Seth and elaborate. "My point is, she's not an easy person to pin down. She seems so plain and yet has this vibrant, sexy home. She's scared and vulnerable, and yet fearless and strong at the same time. She's got enough initiative to hire us, but not enough to go to the cops."

"She hasn't been to the police?" Ronan's voice held shock, but also suspicion.

"Nope. And is very firm about not wanting to as well. Freely admits she's hiding something – something she assures me is unrelated to her being stalked. We're going to have to get it out of her eventually."

"I don't want to doubt her – my gut tells me we can trust her," Seth volunteered, frowning in the direction of the hallway. Vaughn saw him raise his head and sniff, as if he was homing in on her exact location. "We need to be careful," he muttered quietly, and had Vaughn wondering if he was talking to himself or all of them.

Watching their reactions, he decided right then and there to be completely transparent with his partners. "We're going to have to be careful for a number of reasons," he established. "None the least, the fact that she's pretty damn attracted to me – to all of us, if I'm not mistaken."

"What?" Ronan looked shocked, but Vaughn thought there was also a hint of relief and happiness in there too.

"I made sure to get in her way earlier – you know – invade her personal space a little."

"Vaughn!" Ronan reprimanded.

"Oh, relax. You know I wouldn't do anything to hurt her. I just wanted to see what her reaction would be. As we established before, she smells like us. It's pretty damn strange."

"And what did she do?" Seth asked.

"Nearly kissed me, that's what," he replied, rubbing his lips. They were still tingling in anticipation of feeling her skin pressed to his.

"Did you want to kiss her back?" Ronan's voice was quiet.

Vaughn took his time answering. This was tricky

– yes, he wanted to kiss her back, and he also wanted to do much more while he was at it. But he didn't want to hurt his two lovers. Three people together in a relationship may not be commonplace, but there was no mistake – the three of them were committed and had been exclusive for a long time. Hell, he wasn't the most articulate person, but he *was* very much in love with the both of them and couldn't imagine his life without his two panthers. He also couldn't imagine touching anyone else or sharing his men with another – until now.

In fact, his panther was extremely possessive and just the thought of anyone touching Seth or Ronan made him see red. He'd quite happily kill anyone who touched them, be they male or female. They were his. But when he pictured the smaller woman with her soft curves, husky voice, and bowed lips sandwiched between their three bodies as they moved as one, he felt horny as hell.

Both men were watching him intently, awaiting his answer. Given their few previous comments and observations, he was pretty sure they were all on the same page. "Yeah, I wanted to kiss her back. A lot," he admitted, watching them closely for their reactions. "Does that bother you?"

Ronan frowned as Seth shifted uncomfortably,

opening and closing his mouth a couple of times without answering. Vaughn's stomach plunged – had he misjudged the situation and hurt his lovers?

He was about to beg forgiveness when Seth finally spoke, raising clear green eyes to meet his. "No. It doesn't bother me. Not in the slightest," he admitted. "Why is that?" Seth looked his way and then Ronan's. "Ro?"

Ronan was still frowning, but Vaughn could now see that it wasn't in anger – it was his thinking frown – and his pulse began to calm once more. "I feel the same way. Last night, at the bar, when I ushered us all out of there so quickly? It was because my panther and I wanted to jump her bones. I felt guilty as hell."

They all stood in silence, absorbing the information and lost in their own thoughts for a few moments. "Where do we go from here? We're all attracted to her – an oddity considering I haven't gotten it up for anyone but the two of you in years," Vaughn freely confessed.

Ronan shrugged. "Even if we wanted to do something about it, there's no guarantee she'd be interested."

"Oh, she'd be up for it," Vaughn assured them,

remembering the heat in her eyes as she had leaned in for that kiss.

"It doesn't matter if she is." Ronan's voice was firm now. "She's vulnerable at the moment. She's been terrorised for months by some sicko who wants in her pants, and who knows what else. We're here to keep her safe. Nothing more."

"And you think you'll be okay with that?" he asked doubtfully, because he was nothing if not honest. And in truth, he was worried he'd even make it through one evening without wanting to taste Ivory. Especially now that he knew his lovers didn't have a problem with it. They were all on the same page. And then there was that round bed . . .

"I have to be," Ronan responded, but he didn't look convinced.

"Okay, fine. Subject change – what about the other unexpected turn of events?" Seth asked. "She smells like us. That's just fucking weird. What do you think it means?" He turned dark-green eyes towards him. "Could she be a witch from our coven?"

Vaughn hadn't been expecting that. Why the hell would Seth think that? The mere mention of the possibility was jarring. He accepted that Seth still believed there was a member of their coven's bloodline out there somewhere. The kid could believe whatever he wanted. Didn't make it true. But he hated it when Seth kept bringing it up all the time. It was the one thing they ever really fought seriously about.

Luckily, Ronan spoke up, blocking him from his thoughts and his automatic scathing response to Seth's question. "Our coven has never smelt like that before, Seth. Besides, we don't recognise the bloodline through scent. We recognise it through power. And I don't sense even a hint of power on her."

"Then what's with the connection we all feel? It's not just chemistry – I don't just want to screw her. I want to talk to her, get to know her. I want to protect her, make sure she doesn't get hurt. I want to make her happy." His green eyes were darker than usual, and full of confusion. "Isn't that what familiars do for their witches?"

Vaughn reminded himself that Seth had never served a witch before, so his persistence was due to ignorance rather than malice. But this was a touchy subject for Vaughn – and Ronan – and he was beginning to feel twitchy.

Praying for patience, he reasoned with Seth in what he hoped was an even tone. "Ronan is right. The coven's power calls to the panther. Trust us,

Seth, if she were our witch, we would know it beyond a shadow of a doubt." He watched as his young lover's jaw clenched stubbornly and Vaughn knew Seth was going to press the issue. "There is no-one in the bloodline left" – his voice was flat – "and even if there was, do you really think we're just going to stumble across a coven member in some random, podunk town at the bottom of a mountain?"

"Why not?" Seth retorted. "We're going to stumble across them somewhere. Could be here."

His panther stretched inside his mind, gearing up for the perceived fight. He didn't usually mind these battles of the wills with Seth because they invariably led to sex. But now wasn't the time or the place. They had a new client to protect and a new mystery to solve. "Why do you insist on harping on and on about this? This is the second generation Ronan and I have been born into without a single member of the Panthera Coven. The bloodline is extinct. End of story."

"If it was extinct, why was I born? A new familiar with a new soul, bound to serve the Panthera bloodline. If nobody was left, why are we still here? No bloodline means no familiars. We are familiars, therefore there must be a bloodline." Seth peppered him with his argument – an argument he had heard over and over again.

"Will you two stop bickering? This isn't an argument either of you can win. Vaughn, Seth is right on some points and you know it." He turned to Seth, who was looking smug, making Vaughn want to wipe the look right off his handsome face. "And, Seth, Vaughn is right about the magic – we would sense it. There is no way Ivory is any kind of witch, let alone one from our coven."

"Enough of this crap," Vaughn declared. Talking of his lost coven always left him moody for days, and they had work to do. Besides, Ronan was right; it wasn't a dispute either of them could win because neither of them could prove their points. "We need to stop with all our feelings – including the horny ones. We have a job to do. Ivory has a sicko stalking her, and she needs our help. Let's do the job we were hired to do."

"And if she wants more than that?" Seth asked, clearly not willing to give up on the idea of having the pretty little brunette.

"Then that will be up to her, won't it?"

Nine

The second hand on Ivory's bedside alarm clock ticked agonisingly slow. She should be used to the insomnia by now, after having been on high alert for months, lest her prowler paid a nighttime visit. But her restlessness had been for a whole new reason last night. Three whole new reasons, to be exact, and their names were Seth, Vaughn, and Ronan.

The rest of yesterday had been spent answering questions about her routines, her friends, her staff, her family, her hobbies. The only time she hadn't felt like she was being interrogated was when they were dismantling her expensive new alarm and replacing it with their own security system. She now had individual alarms on every window and the external doors, and motion sensors in the house and on her front step. The sensors were hooked up to cameras and would record everything as soon as movement was detected. She was trying not to see it as an invasion of her personal space, but a necessity. It was hard though, given she was such a private person by nature – and, oh yeah, she was hiding the fact that she was a freakin' witch!

Groaning, she rolled onto her back, starfishing on the huge soft mattress. She had purchased the round bed on a whim when she attended a deceased estate auction. Rich, lonely dead people always had the best antiques. It was where she acquired all of her furniture. One look at the decadent and indulgent round bed base had her blowing two months of her income when the gavel came down. She spent weeks eating two-minute noodles after that, but it had been well worth it – even though it was far too big for one person. Hell, it would be too big for two people as well. Now, if there were four people . . .

She yanked her pillow from under her head and did her best to self-suffocate. She had no business thinking those dirty thoughts. Even though the men had been nothing but professional with her and each other the night before, she hadn't missed the easy, intimate way in which they all interacted. Their little ménage looked to be solid and happy. So why did Vaughn have desire in his eyes when he backed her into the wall yesterday? She must have imagined it, she assured herself, and proceeded to get ready for the day.

She found all three of them in the open dining room off the kitchen. She had a large table that could comfortably seat eight people, with single chairs at either end and along one side, and an old church pew along the other. The heavy mahogany table was a priceless, one-of-a-kind, hand-carved piece and had been another steal from a rich dead dude. Although it dominated the space off the kitchen opposite the converted living room, she thought it fit perfectly. It had been her last purchase for her renovated apartment. She wasn't lying when she told Vaughn she had done most of the renovations herself. And she had hardly even cheated with her magic – mostly. Some of the heavier items, like the table and her massive awkwardly shaped bed, had received a little twitch of her nose and wave of her hand.

When she first rolled into Hadleigh, she'd had no intention of staying. The town was too small, with a population of around ten thousand permanent residents. Although, that number almost doubled during all the main holiday periods and during the summer; it was popular for its nature walks, hiking, and rock climbing. Before Hadleigh, she had always chosen to hide out in the bigger cities, believing the old adage that there was safety in numbers. And it had definitely worked, until she started to feel like she was being watched. It was nothing like her pathological gift-giver now, just some raised hairs on the back of her arm every now and again. It was enough to convince her to move on, and she had stumbled upon the picturesque mountain town because she had to pee. One potty stop, one pub purchase, and five years later, she was still here. She absolutely loved it.

She felt a pang of guilt for assuring Vaughn her secret past had nothing to do with the trouble plaguing her now. What if it did? What if it was someone from the conclave? Or even a witch hunter? But if that were the case, surely they wouldn't be trying to scare her with date requests, dead flowers, and soiled lingerie. No – it had to be just some random crazy. But doubt still niggled at her. If it *was* something to do with her magic, the men would be seriously outnumbered and outgunned. But it wasn't like she could tell them she was a modern-day witch. There were still some true

believers out there who were harmless enough –
most of them members of the Wiccan religion –
though they weren't true witches. However, the
majority of people didn't believe in magic, and she
was just as likely to be shipped off to the funny farm
if she confessed now.

"Ivory, you going to stand there all day?"

The deep voice belonged to Seth and had her
jolting from her thoughts. She really had no choice
but to keep on her current path, she decided. So she
pasted a smile on her face and walked to the coffee
machine that appeared to already have gotten a
workout. "Sorry. I was just thinking. I hope everyone
slept well." She turned and leaned back against the
kitchen counter. Damned if the three handsome
men didn't look perfect sitting at her table.

"Sure did, thanks," Ronan answered, looking
fresh and put together. He was clearly a morning
person, and she tried very hard not to hate him
for it.

She cast her eyes over the other two, seeing a
casual looking but somewhat sleepy-eyed Seth and a
grumpy-looking Vaughn. At least one of them wasn't
a fan of mornings. Why wasn't she surprised it was
the blunt, gruff one? "What's the plan for today?" she
asked.

"We'll be with you at work today. You won't be doing much without at least one of us following you around for the foreseeable future, I'm afraid," Ronan informed her – nicely.

"Vaughn said as much yesterday, albeit in a much ruder fashion," she pointed out, causing Ronan and Seth to laugh. Seemed they knew exactly what the other man was like and didn't care. She didn't really mind either, if she were being honest. She always preferred honesty to subterfuge, which was another reason why wearing a false face bugged her. There was only one problem with their plan. "I understand the necessity and I'm very grateful, but I can't just have you prowling around the bar, dogging my every step. I have to work, and people will ask questions."

"We won't get in your way. You'll hardly know we're there at all," Seth assured her.

She eyed them dubiously. They were tall, built, and jaw-droppingly gorgeous, with dangerous auras that screamed bad boy. There was no way they weren't going to stand out like sore thumbs.

"I know what you're thinking, Ivory," Ronan's voice interrupted her thoughts. "But we can blend in when we need to."

She very much doubted that. "This is a small

town," she reminded them. "You won't be able to do much blending. I really don't want the world to know I'm being stalked and need the protection of three bodyguards."

"Because you're keeping secrets," Vaughn pointed out, his voice rough.

She shivered in reaction to his early morning voice despite the accusatory words he was using. Rather than engaging in a verbal sparring match with him, she simply shrugged, taking another sip of the life-affirming coffee in her hand. She saw Ronan cast a dark look towards Vaughn, who merely raised an eyebrow. The man was clearly unrepentant.

"We don't want to tip our hand to your stalker either. If he realises his access to you is being blocked, he will either back off or move up his end game," Ronan explained, ignoring Vaughn's accusation.

She worried her lip – she hadn't considered that having bodyguards would piss off her stalker. "Are you going to be in danger here? Is this guy going to resent your presence enough to try to hurt you?"

"Well, yeah. Hopefully," Seth answered, causing her jaw to drop.

"You want him to come after you?"

Seth shrugged, his shoulders lifting and falling,

drawing her gaze. "It would make life a little easier – draw him out, reel him in, take him out."

He sounded so casual about putting himself in danger. She knew it was their job, but she didn't want to be responsible for putting them in harm's way.

Before she could voice her objections, Ronan chimed back in. "Seth's right. More often than not, just us being here will be enough to force the offender's hand. But it's just as likely that he will take out his rage on you rather than us. That's why it's so important for you to do what we tell you."

She swallowed loudly, unable to suppress a shiver of fear. Whoever it was killed animals and jacked off on underwear. She really didn't want him to focus any more attention on her. She would do her best to follow the instructions and heed the commands of the experts currently taking up residence in her house. But it still didn't solve the problem of their conspicuousness. She didn't care what they said about being able to blend – there was no way her staff wouldn't notice them. Wait a minute . . . her staff . . . An idea hit her.

"What about if I hire you?" she suggested excitedly.

"Um, you kind of already did that," Seth pointed out.

She flapped a hand. "Not in that way. I mean, at the bar? That way no-one would question your presence and you would have a legitimate reason for being there." They all looked at each other and she could practically hear the wheels turning in their heads. They weren't immediately objecting, so she took the opportunity to push the matter. "My head bartender has been at me for months to hire some bouncers." She looked them over once more, trying very hard not to linger on their biceps and pecs. "You certainly look the part."

"Bouncers?" Ronan screwed his nose up in distaste.

"Bouncers, huh?" Vaughn's eyes lit up, the idea obviously appealing to him. "I could do that. Takin' names and crackin' skulls." He rubbed his hands together in glee and she laughed at his exuberance. Of course, he would like the idea of that.

"It's not a bad idea," Seth acknowledged. "Undercover. We've done similar things before."

Ronan looked thoughtful for a moment, and Ivory held her breath. It seemed Ronan was the unofficial leader of their threesome – at least when it came to business matters. Another long moment of contemplation followed before he finally nodded his head. "I think we could make that work. Vaughn and I have actually worked in a pub before anyway."

Excellent, she thought. She had just hired herself three new bouncers.

Ten

Three days later, and nothing of consequence had occurred with regard to her sinister friend. She had received no new packages, no emails, no letters. It was as if he had just up and left . . . or was waiting to drop a bomb. Her nerves were beginning to get the better of her.

Waiting is almost worse than the horrible deliveries, she thought, as she wiped her bar down. It was mid-afternoon and only a handful of patrons graced her tables. Herself, Lee, and Stella – her cook – were the only ones currently working. Oh, other than her new bouncer, of course, she amended, trying to discreetly ogle Seth from across the room.

Her three new bouncers, slash bar staff, had

settled in very easily. It was disconcerting just how easily they integrated into her daily routines. They were right; they could blend when they needed to. Nobody questioned the three men's presence, and Lee was ecstatic to learn they would be doubling as bouncers, as well as helping out behind the scenes. He was more than a little smug when they successfully broke up a fight between three men on their first night. His look was full of 'I told you so,' which she had studiously ignored, of course.

They had received great pleasure upon seeing Trucker Pete's face when he rocked up the night before. The man was completely sober and suitably terrified when he realised the three huge men who he had pissed off were now hanging around on a permanent basis and were in charge of security. She was sure Vaughn, in particular, was gaining some kind of perverse pleasure at making Pete sweat. Libby's eyes bugged out of her head when she had shown up for work their first day. She told Libby the truth, of course, that the three newest Hex employees were actually the private security she recommended. It only made her friend drool more.

The past three days had been spent with at least one of them with her at all times, while the other two utilised their secret bodyguard resources to try

and find her psycho. They'd questioned her relent-
lessly, asking the same questions over and over
again, trying to find any small clue as to the person's
identity. She knew they completed background
checks on everyone in her life – including Trucker
Pete. So far, everyone checked out, much to
Vaughn's irritation. She wasn't any closer to finding
answers, but she did feel safer – despite the fact that
her lust had been on a slow burn for days.

As they asked her questions and got to know her,
she had been doing the same with them. And so far,
she liked everything she heard, from Seth's cheeky
personality to Ronan's intellect, and Vaughn's
grumpy persona. They were truly wonderful men.

"Ivory . . ." Lee was behind her, holding up the
work phone. "Call for you."

He quickly passed the handset over with one
hand, his other already reaching for a glass to pull a
beer. He really was an efficient bartender. She leaned
back against the counter, tucking the phone between
her neck and shoulder, even as she reached for a
glass to buff. Lee wasn't the only one who could
multitask. "Hello?"

"Bad Ivory. Make them leave."

The handset fell to the floor with a clatter along
with her stomach. The voice in her ear was robotic,

but the undercurrent of rage could still be easily heard. It was him. Her stalker. She had never received a phone call before. As sinister and frightening as the notes and parcels were, they still felt somewhat distanced. But hearing a voice made it feel like he was able to reach out and touch her. She shivered, wrapping her arms around herself, and nearly screamed when she felt a muscular arm do the same.

"Seth . . ." she breathed out, recognising his scent almost immediately.

"It's just me," he confirmed. "What's wrong?"

She tilted her head back, looking at him. "How did you know something was wrong?"

"I could smell, err, I could see the look on your face from across the room. Now tell me."

She could have sworn he was about to say he could smell something before changing his mind. Thinking it an odd thing to say, but with bigger worries at the moment, she merely gestured to the handset. Seth picked it up, cursing up a storm when all he heard was a dial tone.

"Come on." He grabbed her hand and dragged her to her office, pushing her into her chair and kneeling in front of her. "Tell me everything."

She shrugged, fiddling with her earrings in a nervous gesture. "It was my mystery admirer. He said I was bad again – must be a running theme of his. He also said, *'Make them leave.'* I assume he was referring to you three."

Seth took her hand, likely saving her from ripping her ear off. "Did you recognise the voice?"

"No. It was robotic. I couldn't even make out if it was male or female," she admitted, realising she kept referring to her stalker as a man when they could just as easily be female.

"What about the tone, the syntax? Remind you of anyone? A jealous ex? A jilted lover?" he pushed, but she was already shaking her head.

"I already told you guys – multiple times. I don't have any recent exes. Hell, the last person to ask me on a date was Lee. And that was months before all of this started."

Seth froze. "Lee? Your bartender?"

She nodded, eyeing him quizzically. He looked pissed for some reason. It was a good look on the man who was always so chilled, she thought.

"Dammit, Ivory! Why didn't you mention this before? A new employee, someone in your close proximity, asked you out, and you rejected him. You didn't think this was important for us to know?"

She laughed before realising Seth was serious. "It

wasn't a big deal. He asked me out once. I said no once. That's it."

"You are not really that naïve, are you?" he asked angrily.

"I'm not naïve and I'm not stupid." Her feminine pride smarted over the lack of faith. "Of course I considered him. But he checked out. Besides, you saw him standing right next to me when the phone rang. It's not Lee."

"What do you mean 'he checked out'? What makes you so sure?" Seth rose to his feet and crossed his arms over his chest, doing a damn fine imitation of Vaughn's cranky face.

"Because I've received packages at times when he hasn't left my sight. It can't be him. Unless I have two stalkers?" Her voice was full of sarcasm.

Seth didn't seem to hear it – or he was ignoring it, for he answered, "No. Stalkers with this kind of pathology tend to work alone. Any kind of competition for your attention would not be tolerated – even from a partner."

She huffed. "I think you're missing the main point here, Seth."

His green eyes widened, forcing his eyebrows up. "I am?"

"Yes." She stood up, placing a hand on his arm. "That was a threat, directed more at you guys than me, I'm thinking. I'm so sorry. I've put you all in danger."

He stared at her seriously for a moment before throwing his head back and laughing uproariously. *What the hell?* Maybe she had been wrong about him. Maybe he was unstable because that was not a normal reaction to learning a psychopath had their sight set on you. "Seth!"

"I'm sorry. You're just so funny, sweetheart. This is what we do for a living. We're supposed to draw out your stalker. If he focuses on us – all the better. We can look after ourselves, trust me." He patted her on the head as if she were a small child or a good little doggie.

She pursed her lips. "Fine."

He had a point, but she was still worried. The thought of any harm coming to her three body-guards made her break out in a cold sweat. *Damn*, she was really getting attached.

"Ivory?"

"Hmm?" She looked up when he said her name, only to take a quick step back. If she didn't know any better, she would have thought there was lust shining in his eyes.

"Thank you for caring about us. It's nice," he smiled, advancing the one step she had retreated.

"I don't care about you," she was quick to defend, before mentally slapping her forehead. That was rude.

"You don't? Well, I'm sorry to hear that. Maybe this will change your mind." He gripped her by the upper arms and lifted her until her face was at the exact same height as his. His lips brushed against hers, once, twice. They were soft and so very warm, and she swayed forwards as if hypnotised . . . only to jerk backwards at the last second, averting sure disaster.

"Put me down," she demanded, and was promptly placed back on her feet. "What is this? I'm not going to be the other woman. Besides, I can't believe you would cheat on your partners," she chastised, telling her foolish heart to stop its crazy beating. He shrugged, the action far too casual for her liking. She was beginning to understand why Seth's laid-back attitude pissed Vaughn off.

"It wouldn't be cheating," he informed her unapologetically. "We've all spoken about it. If any of us were given the opportunity to be with you, it'd be cool with all of us."

"Wait . . . you've spoken about it? You've all

discussed what would happen if I gave you a chance at the goodies?" A part of her was thrilled, while another part of her was pissed at the sheer audacity. The pissed part was winning. She narrowed her eyes. "Let me get this straight—the three of you sat around like some kind of sugar daddies, talking about the best way to get into my pants? Without consulting me?"

Seth's dark-green eyes widened, then his gaze darted around the room, as if he were hoping someone or something would save him. "Um . . ."

"I'm not some kind of sex toy, you know," she informed him primly, despite the evil angel on her shoulder who whispered, *please, please, please make me your sex toy.* "I won't be a passing amusement to three gay men who have suddenly decided they want some salad to go with their meat!"

"Meat? Salad? Say what now?!" He backed up a step under her feminine fury.

"You know what I'm talking about, mister. Maybe you're all a little bored with your carnivorous diet – you want to try being omnivores for a while. Well, this lettuce leaf is onto you, buddy. And she's not buying what you're selling. I won't be used – no matter how tempting."

And it really was tempting, which is why she

spun around quickly, leaving a shell-shocked Seth staring after her in total confusion.

Seth watched the angry swish of Ivory's hips as she stalked from the room. *What the hell just happened?* He didn't think he had ever been reduced to nothing but a walking penis so effectively before. The past three days had been heaven, hell, and purgatory—all at once. The progress of the case was frustratingly slow, but spending time with Ivory had been its own reward. She appealed to him on every level.

He'd always thought Vaughn, Ronan, and himself were all pieces of the one whole; they balanced each other, challenged each other, and complemented each other. He never thought anything was missing before now. But having met the lovely, vulnerable bartender, he was beginning to wonder if there was a bonus piece to their puzzle. A quartet rather than a triad.

He recalled the conversation with Ronan and Vaughn from the night before. They were discussing Ivory – again – and what they wanted to do about her. He felt for sure she was starting to soften towards them. He had no doubts about her lust; the spicy scent of the woman had them walking around with semis twenty-three out of twenty-four hours a day. It was her mind they needed to crack, and he told them as such.

"I'm saying we should make a move. You know, try to woo her, flirt a little."

He paced at the end of the bed Ronan and Vaughn would be sharing that night. He had drawn the short straw to sleep alone . . . again.

"Flirt?! What the hell do I know about flirting? I don't flirt. I don't need to flirt," Vaughn exclaimed indignantly.

"Of course you don't. You just snap those fingers and level those green peepers of yours and thousands fall at your feet," Seth scoffed.

Ronan laughed and Vaughn reached out, cuffing him on the back of the head. But Seth was serious. Of course Vaughn had never had to flirt before. For one thing, he had been so focused on his duty of serving the coven for so long, he never entertained the notion of having a relationship. Seth knew he had been a one-night stand kind of guy and he didn't fault him for that. But it wasn't just duty. Vaughn was absolutely unaware of his own appeal. It was one of the many things Seth loved about him.

"I'm serious, guys. She's flighty, but she's interested. We just need to help get her out of her own way," he said.

He snorted to himself now. Something told him

she was going to be even more in her own way after this little display. Sighing, he sent a quick text to Ronan, telling him and Vaughn to get their butts down here. He needed to update them asap. With any luck, they would be able to trace the call and finally hunt down the crazy arsehole scaring her. And then they would be free to woo Ivory in earnest.

Eleven

The following morning, Ivory stood in front of her coffee machine, fiddling with the settings in frustration.

The stainless steel appliance was a gift from the gods, having been forged in the highest peaks of heaven, she was sure. She was absolutely useless without her morning cup of the bitter brew. Unfortunately, the men had been up before her and changed her pre-set menu. As far as she was concerned, it was an offence punishable by a serious maiming. And if she discovered it was the tallest and broadest of the three men who had touched her baby, she would even consider death as a punishment.

She studiously ignored Seth for the rest of the

day yesterday, finding it hard to look the others in the eye. She couldn't believe Seth had tried to kiss her! And what was worse, she almost let him. The temptation was there, the struggle real, but what she told him was true; she had no intention of being some kind of experiment to them. He had wisely given her space but finally made an attempt to talk to her before she went to bed. He only managed to say her name before she stopped him with a *"Nope. Don't even, buster. Talk to the hand."* Then she flipped him off and retreated to her room. The warm chuckle that followed her down the hallway had her core heating and her lips twitching despite herself. He was incorrigible.

He and Ronan spent the rest of yesterday playing with their computers and trying to trace the ominous call while Vaughn followed Lee around with suspicious eyes, confirming his alibi for all the times she had received packages. She had received remarkably similar reprimands and lectures from all of them when Seth revealed the Lee tidbit. Apparently, she had committed some major faux pas by neglecting to mention the non-date. She still believed they were focusing on the wrong thing and had once again mentioned her concerns. Vaughn had grunted, rolling his eyes, whilst Ronan had thanked her for her worry in the kindest of terms. She had seen his lips twitching, though, and found it just as infuriating as Seth's hilarity and Vaughn's disdain. They seemed to think they were invincible.

Vaughn emerged from the spare bedroom, looking fit and handsome, and okay – maybe a little invincible. He was wearing dark denim jeans and a plain black T-shirt that made his bright-green eyes pop in the early morning light. "Good morning, Ivory."

She narrowed her eyes at him. Usually, she only received a grunt for the first fifteen minutes he was awake. He was almost as bad as her with the coffee machine. "Good morning," she responded slowly.

"How did you sleep?" he asked, nudging her out of the way. He pressed two buttons and had her baby purring under his competent hands in seconds. She forced herself not to scowl at the traitorous machine. Even her coffee maker responded sweetly to the man.

"Not too bad," she replied truthfully. After her initial shock of hearing that robotic voice yesterday, and being told she was 'bad' yet again, she had actually felt some relief. Those few days of just waiting for the other shoe to drop had been horribly tense.

And the men now had something extra to work with. "Were you able to trace the call?"

Vaughn scowled, and she had the insane urge to smooth out his furrowed forehead with her fingers. "It was from a no-plan phone that had already been disconnected. It's completely untraceable, so it's another dead end. Same as Lee. He's alibied up to his eyeballs and was suitably confused and intimidated when I cornered him yesterday."

"Vaughn!"

"What?" he asked, all innocent.

She merely rolled her eyes. The man was so exasperating. As long as her best bartender didn't quit on her, it would be fine.

"Here you go. Your sacred beverage, m'lady." She could have sworn Vaughn winked at her as he handed her a steaming mug, made just the way she liked it.

She eyed him warily. "Do you have a twitch or something?"

She saw his jaw clench before he took a deep breath, as if deliberately trying to relax. "No. You look lovely this morning, by the way."

She looked down at herself. She was wearing her normal work uniform of black jeans but had gone all out and put on a black button-up shirt rather than a plain black tee. She was beginning to get worried; Vaughn was never this chipper. Maybe he was having a stroke? "Are you feeling okay?"

"I feel fine," he growled, slamming his own coffee mug down on the counter.

Now that was more like it. "What are you doing, then?"

He spun to face her quickly. "I'm flirting with you."

She swore she felt her jaw literally hit the floor. "You are?" she squeaked.

He huffed irritably. "Well, if you have to ask, I'm obviously not doing it right."

She fought a smile—he was almost pouting. Vaughn never pouted. She cleared her throat. "That's not what I meant. I mean, why are you flirting with me?"

"Because I like you." The statement was sweet in its simplicity. "And because Seth told us how you went all feminist on him when he hit on you yesterday. We all thought we should woo you, flirt with you – that kind of crap."

Sweet? Had she really just thought this blunt, boorish buffoon was sweet just seconds ago? "First, I did not go all 'feminist' on Seth – and be careful," she warned, "that kind of comment will get you kicked in the balls. I simply informed him of the error of his ways regarding men's thinking and women's sexuality."

He snorted. "The way I hear it, you informed him of the error of his ways regarding wanting to add a little foliage to his all-protein diet."

"Second"—she raised her voice, deliberately ignoring his interruption—"I'll have you know that flirting is a common and effective part of courtship."

He crossed his impressive arms over his impressive chest, looking entirely unconvinced. "Waste of time, if you ask me."

It probably was to him, she acknowledged. She doubted he had ever had to work for attention or affections. Legions probably swooned at his feet with the crook of a finger – pre- Seth and Ronan, of course. The thing that really confused her though, was why he would choose to try his pathetic wooing techniques on her. Oh, she knew what Seth said; they had *discussed* their shared desire of her. Even if she believed them, there were easier ways for them to get her into bed. Seduction being the biggie. Seduction was all about the physical desire. She had no doubt they could seduce the underwear off her in a matter of minutes if they tried. Flirting, on the other hand, was more about the mental and emotional desire – encouraging the person to enjoy you as a person, and not just as a sex object.

She shook her head, admitting, "I don't understand you – any of you."

"What's to understand?"

How could she make him see her perspective when he was just so practical? "You love Ronan and Seth."

He nodded, no hesitation. "I do. Very much."

"And yet, you say you like me," she pointed out.

Another decisive nod. "I do. Very much."

"How do you reconcile those two things?" she asked, truly curious about his response.

He eyed her thoughtfully, asking his own question instead of answering hers. "Why do women have to make things so complicated?"

"Vaughn!" she growled, thoroughly annoyed with him. But he grabbed her arm before she could spin away.

"Wait a minute. Let me ask you this: do you like me?"

"Not at the moment," she assured him, glaring daggers in his direction.

He merely chuckled – a wholly appealing sound. "I'll take that as a yes. And do you like Ronan and Seth? Be honest," he warned.

"Yes," she sighed. "I like Ronan and Seth too."

"So you like all of us." It was a statement.

"Yes."

"At the same time," he clarified.

She huffed. "Yes. At the same time. But—"

"No buts. Why with the but? There will be no more buts. I like all of you at the same time too. Just like how I like bacon and ice cream at the same time."

He said that as if it made complete sense. "Bacon and ice cream?"

"Yes. Salty and sweet. Cold and hot. They don't oppose each other; they complement each other. It's delicious and you should try it, but that's not the point."

"What is the point again?" she rubbed her forehead. Was that a headache brewing?

"This," he answered, before reaching out, reeling her in, and capturing her lips with his own in one seamless motion.

Any protest died the moment his tongue met her own – dancing and duelling and seducing. He tasted spicy and fresh and exciting. Her arms rose up of their own volition, her hands threading through the thickness of the silky strands of his blond hair. He wrapped his arms around her, one large hand spanning the width of her lower back as the other boldly cupped her bottom. He lifted her higher, as if he couldn't get close enough, and she moaned, arching her back and pressing her tingling breasts against the firmness of his chest. Her breathing got faster and faster—so much so, she was becoming dizzy. Worried she might make a total fool of herself by passing out from the sheer pleasure of just his lips against her own, she pulled back, putting an inch of space between them.

"Oh . . ." was about all she could articulate.

"You can say that again."

Vaughn's words had her looking up into his intense green eyes. They were glazed and dazed, and just a little bit feverish. His chest was pumping as if he had run a marathon and there was a fine tremor in the hands that still held her so securely. It seemed she wasn't the only one to be thoroughly over-whelmed by the experience. The knowledge made her feel strong, and a saucy smile pulled at her lips. Making a big man tremble was hot as hell.

"What's that smile about, little witch?"

And just like that, the flames of lust were extin-guished.

She stepped out of his arms. "What did you call me?"

His brows furrowed in concern, clearly confused and worried over her reaction. "That smile – it was sexy, seductive . . . secretive. Made me think of a witch." He paused as if struggling to find the right words, before sighing and running his hands through his dishevelled hair. "It was supposed to be an endearment. Next time I'll use 'sweetheart,' how about that?"

Her heart rate began to slow again upon hearing his explanation. A term of endearment. That was all. He couldn't have known just how right he was, and just how much his words hit home. She must have been silent for too long, for he sighed loudly, the sound full of male aggravation.

"You're thinking too hard again."

Maybe she was. But hearing the word 'witch' on his lips had acted as a stark reminder that she was trying to hide here. That the whole reason Vaughn was even in her life at the moment was because she had someone stalking her and threatening the life she had built for herself. She couldn't afford to forget that. "I'm sorry. That was a mistake."

Anger leaped in his eyes at her words. "Bullshit. We were so hot together, I thought we were going to spontaneously combust. You liked it. I know you did."

"I'm not denying that." *Or the heat I felt in his arms*, she acknowledged to herself. "But I'm your client. You're here to do a job. We shouldn't complicate things. We need to stay focused."

Truth, she assured herself. *That was all true*. But her words seemed to piss him off even more, if the stiffening of his shoulders and the rumble in his chest were any indication.

He stepped close, invading her personal space for an entirely different reason than moments before. "My first priority is keeping you safe. I would never do anything to jeopardise your safety – none of us would. Never doubt that."

She swallowed, feeling a little ashamed. She didn't doubt that. They were men of honour with strong protective drives, champions for those weaker than themselves and defenders of justice. She felt safer with them than she had anywhere in her whole life, and she had no doubt they would discover who was tormenting her and eliminate the threat. Her only problem was, she was terrified they would discover what she was hiding too. And then they would hate her – or worse – fear her. Witches? Magic? The supernatural world tended to freak out most people.

Needing to soothe her insult, she placed a gentle

hand on his rigid arm. "I know that, Vaughn. I trust all of you to keep me safe without reservation."

His narrowed eyes studied her intently as if gauging the sincerity of her words, before he finally nodded. "Well, that's something at least. This isn't a habit of ours, you know. We don't mix business with pleasure, seducing every client we meet. You're special."

You're special. Why should two simple words have tears threatening to break free? Was she so starved for affection? Probably, she admitted. It had been years since she heard anyone utter those words and actually mean them. Her mother had told her she was special and wanted and loved every single day. When she died twelve years ago and Ivory was forced to hide on her own, she was careful to keep a certain emotional distance in every relationship she entered—including her friendships. Libby was the first real best friend Ivory had ever allowed herself, and even now, she was still lying to her.

"Vaughn . . ." She trailed off, unsure of what she wanted to say.

"Just give me a chance," he implored, seeing an opening. "Give *us* a chance."

She smiled a little at that. "Us, huh?"

He held her gaze, his expression guileless. "Yeah.

Us. We're a package deal – you have to know that. Admittedly, Ronan and Seth aren't much in the looks or personality department, but I've learned to live with it. I'm sure you can too."

His teasing startled a laugh out of her. "Look at you – making funnies. And you say you don't know how to flirt."

He looked surprised. "That was flirting?"

She laughed again, enjoying him – enjoying them together, if she was being totally honest. It was entirely too tempting to engage with him like this – casual, friendly, and with a hint of sexual tension underpinning it all. Too bad she couldn't keep him, or his proposed package deal.

Twelve

T wo days later, Ivory had to force her eyes from straying in the direction of her three new housemates. They were currently flanking the door like buff sentinels in jeans, plain tees, and military boots. She wanted to use them all like a scratching post.

After the explosive kiss she had shared with Vaughn, she expected things to become uncomfortable. But dinner with the three of them the evening before was surprisingly easy, with them all sharing embarrassing stories about each other. It was as funny as it was enlightening. She spent the past couple of nights pondering her current situation, and whether or not she should take them up on their offer and get her flirt on.

"Well?"

Ivory jerked, spinning to find Libby standing directly behind her. Libby just had four rostered days off in a row, and Ivory had seen it as a blessing. Having Libby and her mouth spouting off every damn thing that popped into her head would have been an absolute nightmare to contain. Looking at her cool-blue eyes that were lit with humour but also cheekiness, Ivory decided to play dumb. *Admit nothing, Ivory.* "Well, what?" she asked, feigning ignorance.

Libby rolled her eyes. "Don't be obtuse, Ivory. The Three Musketeers have been sleeping at your place for a week now. Have there been any . . . sword fights?" She waggled her eyebrows outrageously.

Ivory burst out laughing. "You're terrible!"

Libby shrugged, unrepentant. "That's why you love me."

Ivory smiled at her closest friend. She did indeed love her, and Libby was also very smart and supportive – when that evil tongue of hers didn't get in the way. Maybe she could help her figure out the conundrum that was three delicious bodyguards. Possibly talk her out of her insane fantasies and the urgings for the men. She sighed. "There were no sword fights – none that involved me, anyway."

"Why the hell not? Those men are absolutely gorgeous, and it's clear you still all have some chemistry. If even one of them looked at me like all of them look at you, I'd have had them branded and caged by now. Libby's love slaves for all eternity."

Ivory chuckled at her exuberant friend. "Well, that's one of the obvious problems, isn't it? There are three of them, *three!*"

Libby merely sighed, gazing poignantly off into the distance for a moment. "I know." She looked back at Ivory. "Ain't it grand?"

Goodness, yes! She responded silently. It was indeed very grand, but she couldn't admit that out loud. "It's not exactly the done thing, Lib. I can't just get it on with three men at the same time."

"Why the hell not?"

"Come on, Lib. Be serious," she said. She had been hoping her friend would talk her down off the cliff. Instead, it seemed like she wanted to push her off! She should have known better.

"I am serious. Why does it matter if there are three of them?" she demanded. "The more the merrier, I say."

Ivory snorted. "Yeah, *you* say. But society doesn't say that. If I slept with all of them at the same time, I'd be a slut."

"Who gives a fuck what society thinks? And you are so far from a slut, it's laughable. Besides, if I'm not mistaken, those boys are already in a relationship. Do you think they're sluts?"

"Of course not!" she responded, immediately defending them. "They're in a committed relationship – a loving one from what I've seen. They're happy and not hurting anyone. I'd never put a negative label on that kind of love."

"Uh huh." Libby nodded, looking all smug.

Damn. She had just successfully torpedoed her own argument. Libby was a shifty little waitress! "Okay then. I don't have a problem with polyamorous relationships – you got me there. But how about the other obvious issue? I mean, look at them and look at me. What could they possibly want with me other than a passing amusement? I may be staring down the celibacy barrel, but I'm not so desperate I'll let myself be used as some kind of plaything."

Libby let out an aggrieved sound and faced her more fully. Placing her hands on Ivory's cheeks, she spoke firmly, "Bestie, you listen to me; you are beautiful. I don't know what douche made you believe you weren't, but you need to get over that. And even if you weren't much to look at, looks aren't everything. A person's true beauty comes from within. I thought you had more self-esteem than this."

Ivory flinched guiltily. Her problem with her looks didn't come from an arsehole ex, as Libby assumed. And truly, she didn't mind the face she'd chosen to help hide her away from the world – she really wasn't that vain or self-obsessed. What she hated was the constant lie. She hated that no-one ever saw the true her. She wanted to be able to look at her friend and see her through her own unique violet irises. She wanted those three men to look at her face and see her real cheekbones, fantasise about her real lips, and dream about stroking her real hair. It wasn't self-doubt she felt, but longing.

"You're right, Lib," was all she could say.

"Damn right I am. Now, have any of them made you feel cheap or like a temporary romp between the sheets?"

Ivory sighed. "No. In fact, they're saying all the right things."

"Then why don't you listen?" Libby asked earnestly.

"It's not that simple." But she was wavering . . .

"So make it simple." Libby had an answer for everything.

"They're here to do a job. Even if I allowed something to happen, they'll be moving on as soon as my freaky stalker is caught. I really don't want to be some weekend fling – not with them."

"Well now, that's interesting. I know for a fact you haven't minded being a weekend fling in the past. There must be something different about them."

There was. Ivory didn't know what, but there was definitely something about the trio that drew her in. They made her want, and they made her need. For the first time in her life, she felt . . . lonely. Never before had she felt her life was lacking in any way. She was happy – as much as she could be while hiding her true nature. She had a home, a business, friends. She had lovers when she chose, and she went on vacations. But ever since meeting the three men, she had begun to feel like she was missing something – something she couldn't name. It bothered her and it also made her yearn.

Not wanting to admit any of that out loud, she asked instead, "Why are you pushing this so much?"

Libby frowned for a moment before answering, "I just want to see you happy, Ivory. You've been so good to me – giving me this job when I had no references. You . . ." she paused, seeming to choke up a little, ". . . really have been a good friend to me."

Ivory slung an arm over her shoulder, rubbing it in comfort, not sure why the other woman was being so sentimental, but appreciating it nonetheless. "You've been a good friend to me too. If it weren't for you, I'd probably be some kind of weird old pub owner with three cats and a cactus collection."

Libby laughed. "You do have a tendency to become a recluse if I don't prod you."

Ivory knew she did – it was just part of her nature. She was independent and treasured her solitude, but she also enjoyed being social. Sometimes she would forget that – until Libby reminded her by taking her out.

"If you're not willing to listen to me or to them – even when we're all saying the right things – listen to your gut. Trust your instincts. Please?" Libby asked.

Ivory nodded. "Okay, okay. I'll go with my gut."

"And your loins. Go with them too," Libby added, causing them both to dissolve into hysterical laughter. She really was a gem. "And remember: why choose if you don't have to?" Lib added with a wink.

Ivory simply shook her head, glancing in the direction of her 'bouncers.' They must have felt her eyes on them, for all three of them stopped talking and looked up as one. Whoa, talk about potent. Three sets of eyes in varying shades of jade pinned her to the spot, and she swore she could hear her own heartbeat as it began a frantic rhythm. She was so hyper-aware of them at all times. It didn't help that they had all upped their 'flirt with Ivory' agenda. Not only did it include steamy looks and playful banter, but they had also started touching her. Just casual touches—light brushes of their arms against hers as she walked past, and hands meeting as she passed them their morning coffee.

As she watched, Seth jerked his head in a 'come here' gesture. She looked behind her, pretending to look for someone else. When she turned back around, Seth pointed at her and then pointed at the ground in front of him. She mimed an amazed 'who me?' as she clutched her hands to her chest. They all looked surprised at her antics, and the warm pleasure she saw on their faces made her feel like a real heel. Had she been such a tough nut that some lame miming made them happy? Man, she really was a bitch. Well, no more, she decided, picking her way through the crowd in their direction. She was going to open her mind and take a chance on this once-in-a-lifetime opportunity.

"Ivory!" Lib yelled from behind her. She paused,

looking back to see her crazy friend holding up two fingers on either hand and crossing them over each other. She didn't speak, but Ivory had no trouble reading the "hashtag why choose?" in her exaggerated lip movements.

Ivory shook her head, refusing to be baited and refusing to smile as she wanted to – she really shouldn't encourage her.

"Did she just hashtag you?"

Ivory glanced up, her breath catching in her chest a little when she saw Seth's smiling face directly in front of her. "Ignore her. She's nuts."

"She's fun," he retorted.

Well, she couldn't dispute that.

"Are you done for the night?" Ronan asked from her left.

"Yes. Libby, Lee, and Craig are working close tonight." It was eleven now, and she had been working for twelve hours.

"Good. I'm starving." Seth expelled a pent-up breath.

Vaughn rolled his eyes. "You're always starving."

Seth narrowed his eyes back. "I'm a growing boy."

"Well, you won't be doing any more growing tonight. You're on bouncer duty," Vaughn reminded him, with a tad too much relish.

Seth's shoulders immediately slumped and all the animation on his face disintegrated in an instant. They had decided that at least one of them would be with her at all times in her apartment, and two of them when she was out in public. Not that she went out in public much other than here lately. She could still hear that chilling voice in her head telling her she was bad and to make them leave. She didn't think walking around town with all three of them on her arm would help the situation. Tonight, both Vaughn and Ronan would be with her upstairs, and Seth would stay and play the part of bouncer. It was too suspicious if they all left when she did. There were only four hours left until everything shut down for the night – not that Seth seemed to care about that. The man was pouting big time.

"Why do you both get to play with Ivory while I stay here?" he sulked.

"Because you lost the rock off, ya big baby," Vaughn taunted, nudging his shoulder.

Ivory giggled at that. It seemed the only way the three of them were ever able to make any fair decision was to engage in a round of rock, scissors, paper. She watched them complete the ritual every night before bedtime to determine who would be on night duty, and who would be sharing the bed or sleeping alone. Poor Seth seemed to lose with alarming regularity.

"It's only spag bol, Seth. Nothing exciting. I promise to save some for you." She actually enjoyed cooking for them every night. She loved cooking and baking, and it was nice to see someone other than herself reaping the benefit of her culinary skills.

"That's not the point. They're going to try to steal you from me." He placed his hand over his heart dramatically.

She laughed. "There's plenty of me to go around."

Shocked stillness met her words. Crap. She'd just said that out loud. It had been her first honest response to their advances, and she wouldn't take it back. No matter what those crazy butterflies in her stomach thought.

Vaughn's face looked earnest as he demanded confirmation. "Is there?"

She swallowed. *All in, Ivory.* "Yes. There is," she pledged.

Thirteen

Ronan had been unable to take his eyes off Ivory the whole night. Her comfort level with them had grown by leaps and bounds over the past few days and although she had been easy with them, she had yet to reciprocate their obvious advances. But this evening he had noticed a definite shift in her temperament.

She was always easy-going and laid back in general, but he sensed she was never fully relaxed around them. However, since they had returned to her apartment above the bar, she'd been playful, and her banter held definite sexual undertones. He wanted to grab her and kiss her senseless but was afraid this new little bubble would pop.

The past week had been one of the happiest of

his life – despite the terrible and inappropriate circumstances. The more he learned about their feisty little client, the more he liked. And he knew he wasn't alone in his crush either. Seth and Vaughn were just as interested and intrigued. She was a true dichotomy, feminine and vulnerable but also strong and independent. She had been making her own way in the world since her mother died when she was eighteen and wasn't used to asking for help from anyone. She was always happy to talk about her past, including adventures, education, and travels, in broad terms but never specifics. It was the only blight on his infatuation.

Even though they had long since stopped worrying about her being a hunter, they all knew she was still keeping something from them. He hoped this new, open Ivory would soon trust them enough to share. It was almost a full-time job keeping Vaughn's blunt, suspicious mouth shut. The man and his panther were practically frothing at the mouth to make Ivory talk. But at the end of the day, it really wasn't any of their business unless Ivory decided it was.

He pushed back the bowl he had practically licked clean and patted his full stomach. It was now well past one in the morning, and they were only just finishing up another delicious home-cooked meal. Ivory had ended up staying downstairs for another hour and by the time they completed their usual checks and Ivory showered and cooked, it made their dinner more like a midnight snack. Not that he was complaining – none of them could cook worth shit – so he was basking in all these wonderful meals.

"What's this?" He looked askance at the bowl Ivory placed in front of him.

"Dessert," was her prompt reply, placing an identical bowl in front of Vaughn.

Ronan picked up his spoon and prodded Ivory's offering dubiously. It looked to be Neapolitan ice cream, which was fine, he loved all three flavours. But what was strange was the topping. It was brown in colour, but he knew it wasn't chocolate. Inhaling deeply, he picked up the salty and greasy smell of bacon. *Bacon?* He groaned. This strange concoction was a favourite of Vaughn's – he had somehow shanghaied Ivory into making it for him.

Ronan moaned. "Bacon and ice cream?"

She nodded, staring at Vaughn intently. "Yes. It's the best of both worlds."

Desire, heady and intense started to pump off Vaughn in waves. Clearly, Ronan was missing something here. And it was something *big* he realised, as Vaughn pushed his seat back from the table, paced to Ivory in two quick strides, scooped her off her feet, and proceeded to kiss the living hell out of her. For her part, Ivory didn't push him away or slap his face, or any of the things Ronan assumed she would. He sat, dumbfounded and horny, watching the show until Vaughn returned a swaying Ivory to her feet some minutes later.

"We're kissing now? Kissing is allowed? Since when is kissing allowed?" He really hoped he didn't sound as childish to the others as he did to his own ears.

Ivory giggled – actually giggled. "Since now."

That was all the confirmation he needed. Surging from his own chair, he grabbed her around the waist and kissed her with all the pent-up passion he'd been bottling up since meeting her. He moaned because her lips were just as soft as he imagined, groaned because her tongue reached out to caress his, and growled because her unique flavour burst across his taste buds in an intoxicating mix of sweetness, fresh-ness, and wildness. She tasted exactly the way she smelled. Her soft curves aligned perfectly with his hard frame, and he had to fight his panther's instinct to lay her across the table and have *her* for dessert.

Unfortunately, oxygen soon became a necessity, and he pulled back, watching her parted lips and closed eyes with satisfaction. She ducked her head and cleared her throat, putting some space between them. Although she had been as into it as he was, she was now looking a little shy and uncomfortable. That wouldn't do.

Hoping to break the tension, he sat back down and picked up his spoon. "Okay, it's official. I want bacon and ice cream every meal from now on."

His joke had the desired effect, causing a laugh to bubble in her chest and Vaughn to snort in appreciation.

They were just scraping the bottom of their bowls with their spoons when Seth walked in more than an hour before he was expected. Ronan was surprised at how much he had enjoyed the salty and sweet treat – not that he would ever admit that to Vaughn. The man had been trying to get him to taste his weird concoction for years.

"There he is." Ronan didn't need to look up to see the smile on Ivory's face. He could hear it in her voice and truly believed they had turned a corner with her this evening. "The third musketeer. We were just – what is it?"

He looked up sharply when Ivory's tone changed

from happy to guarded. Seth's face was as serious as he had ever seen it. But there was also something else – rage, Ronan thought, standing from his seat. Seth was furious about something.

"A customer just walked up to me and handed me this." He held up a plain, familiar envelope between two fingers. "Said he found it stuck to the closed front door, saw it was addressed to Ivory, and handed it in. He's a local – didn't seem to be lying," he added, nodding in their direction to communicate that his panther hadn't scented a lie. The good Samaritan wasn't their guy.

"What does it say this time?" Ivory demanded, but Ronan could hear the nerves underneath her strong tone.

Seth hesitated, and Ronan knew it must be bad. He stood next to Ivory, placing his hand on her right shoulder. Vaughn mirrored his actions on her left side. He gave a small nod, indicating Seth should show her. It was their job to protect her but not to shield her – no matter how much they wanted to. Seth handed the envelope over and Ivory opened it up, shrugging out of their grip. All Ronan had been able to make out was that there were multiple pieces of paper enclosed.

Ivory let out a thin whine, dropping the envelope

and scattering its contents all over her beautiful mahogany table. She dashed from the room, and he heard the slam of the bathroom door before obvious sounds of retching reached his ears. Bending down, he picked up the images and instantly felt his canines extend and his claws explode from his fingertips.

"I'm going to kill him. When we find this fucker, he's dead," he snarled.

Ivory spent a good ten minutes emptying the contents of her stomach. Her delicious meal of spaghetti bolognese and her new favourite dessert didn't taste so good coming back up. The men knocked on the door, asking if she was okay and could they come in. She managed to garble a bunch of unintelligible words and lock the main bathroom door, before sliding down onto the tile and allowing herself to have a decent crying jag. Blessedly, they let her be, but not before assuring her they were finding and removing the cameras.

The *cameras.* She firmed her jaw again when more tears threatened to spill. She had never felt so exposed or violated in her whole life. The envelope held multiple photos of her in her own en suite. She was naked in every one of them – in the shower, brushing her teeth, lathering body lotion over herself. That was violation enough, but what had dinner rushing up her oesophagus was what had been done to the photos. In each and every one, there were scratches, cuts, hacks, or lewd scribbles over her breasts and genitals. Whoever was stalking her had metaphorically mutilated her. What started out as someone wanting a harmless date had devolved into someone wanting to maim her sexually.

She was in a state of shock. Who could possibly hate her that much? Or, what was worse, who could believe they loved her that much? That amount of sexual rage had to stem from a fine line between love and hate.

"Ivory . . ." Seth's voice reached her ears through the wooden door despite the tentative quality of it.

She scrubbed shaking hands over her face, refusing to look in the mirror and see how much of a wreck she looked like; her fair skin did not react well to tears. She opened the door to find all three of them standing on the threshold. She couldn't look them in the eye yet, though. They had all seen those photos, and she felt absolutely humiliated.

"How many did you find?" she asked, knowing

there must have been more than one camera because the photos portrayed her from multiple angles.

"Two in the en suite, one in the shower cubicle, one above the sink. There was also one above your bed." Vaughn sounded like he was chewing on gravel. His voice was so low and gruff she could barely understand him.

Looking around, she saw identical expressions of rage on Seth and Ronan's faces as well. She figured when her three bodyguards got their hands on the sick fucker doing this, he would be a dead man within seconds.

"We're so sorry, Ivory. We know it's unforgivable of us but—"

"Wait, what are you talking about?" *What could they possibly have to be sorry for?*

"When we arrived, we swept your place for bugs and anything that gave off an electrical charge. There was no sign of anything like that. But they must have already been in place. The three cameras we found were small and sophisticated. They ran on a timer or an external remote, rather than being turned on all the time. It's why we missed them. But that's no excuse. We are so sorry." Ronan's expression was pained, as if someone had kicked him in the nuts or something. He looked positively green.

"Stop, Ronan. This isn't on you guys. I don't want to hear that kind of crap. There's one person who is to blame for all this. It's that sick—" she broke off, her breath hitching. "He's been in my house. How could I not have known? And did you see what he did to me? He cut into—" Her words dropped off again as panic climbed up her throat, cutting off her airways.

Immediately and as one, the three men surrounded her, closing in from all sides, a solid wall of warmth and muscles. She let herself just lean, knowing they would support her. The thought of some stranger watching her in her bedroom – in her shower – made her feel sick. She trembled a little and felt multiple sets of hands pat at her in comfort. Multiple voices murmured nonsense words in order to soothe. Thank goodness she had them. Thank goodness they were here to protect her and make her strong, and . . .

Ivory stiffened at her inner monologue as much as her fearful actions. Since when did she tremble? Since when did she need a man, let alone three, to make her strong? This man, this stranger, had made her weak – made her soft. Her mother had raised her to be a strong, independent woman. Sure, she taught her to know her weaknesses, but also to never give in to them. She told her to rise above her weaknesses, to fight them and to turn them into strengths. Ivory had built her business from the ground up. She had also renovated her home, from installing the toilet to painting the ceilings.

She was capable. She was strong. She was a frigging witch, for god's sake! And she had allowed some nameless, faceless bastard to make her feel vulnerable – make her question herself like never before. Six months ago, if a pack of gorgeous men invited her into their bed, she would have skipped into it, singing "Joy to the World." But now? She was overthinking, making excuses, doubting herself. They knew she was keeping secrets, but these men still trusted her, still wanted her. She was the one not trusting them. She was the one with the doubts and the insecurities. It made her hate her anonymous stalker even more. She had made a good start by flirting, and allowing Vaughn and Ronan to kiss her senseless earlier, but she wanted more.

With her fear falling away and righteous anger taking its place, she decided it was time to stop being a puppet and turn her weakness into strength.

Fourteen

"It's okay, Ivory. We won't let anyone hurt you," Ronan's voice assured her.

So it was Ronan directly in front of her then. A comforting hand ran down her back and she recognised it by the size – that was Seth behind her. That meant the muscled arm wrapped tightly around her waist from the side must belong to Vaughn.

Opening her eyes and peering up, she met Ronan's gaze, which was full of concern and anger . . . but also desire. It was always there, like a low simmer, bubbling away in the background. Well, it was time to bring that simmer to a boil.

She gave a hard tug on the fabric currently bunched in her hands and stole a kiss full of passion and want as soon as Ronan's lips were within touching distance. She heard a moan – wanton and needy – and knew the aching sound had come from her. Ronan kissed her back feverishly as hands other than his own roamed up her sides before cupping her breasts. She pulled back, only so she could moan some more and push herself more fully into the large palms that were igniting her inner flames. Her head fell back, landing on Seth's broad chest as he continued to shape and mould, plucking at her now-hard nipples every few seconds. She felt his lips against her neck and couldn't contain the shiver that slid over her body when he tugged a sensitive earlobe into his mouth playfully.

Hands on her hips had her refocusing on Vaughn, who'd moved in front of her, eyes shining like emeralds. His head lowered to capture her mouth even as he shoved a muscled thigh between her legs, encouraging her to move. *Yes, friction*, she thought giddily, eagerly moving her hips in time with his urging hands. She had begun to grow damp the second Ronan's lips touched her own. Now, with Seth's mouth at her neck and Vaughn's against hers as three sets of hands forged leisurely tracks over her body, she knew she could come from this alone. But she wanted more. She wanted flesh.

She slid her hands under Vaughn's shirt, her palms heating immediately upon feeling the textured hardness of fine hairs over rigid muscle. She pushed the material upward, only to be blocked when it bunched under his armpits. "Arms. Lift," she demanded, and felt more than heard the rumble of laughter in Vaughn's chest. All it served to do was draw her eyes back to the firm, tanned skin stretched so tightly over his abs. "*Now*, Vaughn," she ordered again, when he failed to do as she bid.

Large hands captured her frenzied ones, and she deigned to look up. Vaughn's face was tight with passion . . . but also with control. "Ivory, wait," he said, and she had the absurd urge to growl at him. She didn't want to wait. She had been waiting. She wanted her men, and she wanted them now.

She shook her head. "More," was all she said.

"Ivory, we don't want to pressure you."

The voice came from behind her and belonged to Seth, his hands shifting from her aching breasts to her hips. She whimpered in frustration, pushing herself harder against Vaughn's thigh. "Yes, pressure. More pressure."

But strong hands held her still, compounding her exasperation – but also fuelling her lust. Those hands were mighty strong. What she wouldn't give to feel them holding her down, arms pinned above her head by one of them, ankles held in a similar fashion by another, as the last of them pounded into her while she was completely at their mercy.

"Holy fuck."

"Jesus Christ."

"Mercy."

She glanced around, confused at the various expletives, as well as the multiple groans. "What?"

"Ivory, you basically just told us you wanted to be pinned down while we fucked you into oblivion," Seth panted out from behind her.

"Did I actually say that?" she enquired sheepishly. A blush heated her cheeks even though she wasn't really embarrassed. She may as well be up front.

"Yes!" all three men answered at once. Apparently, they were all a little on edge.

She shrugged. "Oops."

"Oops? Ivory . . ." Ronan, clearly agitated, ran his fingers through his thick, lush hair. She wanted to do the same. "You've had a scare, and you're upset. We don't want to take advantage of you," he explained, cupping her face. "We want to take care of you."

Take care of her? Nuh uh. What did they not understand about oblivion and fucking? She was taking her power back. Seeing the sincere but unsure looks on the men's faces made her feel a little bit bad for them. Poor men. They had no idea what they were in for. She took three slow steps back, disentangling herself from six arms. She ran her fingers over the buttons of her shirt before slipping them through their holes, slowly revealing the emerald-green, lacy bra beneath. She may not have been able to walk around with her true face, and her work required practical clothing, but underneath it all, she indulged in an extensive array of luxurious lingerie. She loved seeing the bold colours against her skin and feeling the slide of satin or silk underneath her clothes. The matching set she had put on that morning was a new favourite. She had become rather partial to the colour green over the past week.

She allowed her shirt to fall from her shoulders, three sets of eyes following the movement and making her feel wanted, cherished. She moved her hands over her bare stomach, circling the jewel in her belly button, before unbuttoning and unzipping her black jeans. Her hands ran over her hips, pushing the denim down, and she gave her butt a shimmy at the same time – more to get the material moving rather than to be enticing. Apparently, it had the same effect, though, for all three men groaned and shifted restlessly. Shaking out her brown hair and wishing it was her natural white colour, she straightened so the trio could get a gander at the matching low-cut lace boy legs she wore. She loved the flattering way the little shorts cupped her butt, riding high on her thighs. She may hide her powers and face from the world, but her body of curves and pale skin was all hers – no magic added.

Eyeing Seth, Ronan, and Vaughn, she could see they were holding onto their control by a thread, but also not wanting to make the first move either. Looked like they needed a little more encouragement. "So . . . who wants first dibs?"

She laughed at the stampede that followed: jostling bodies, pushing and shoving, good-natured swearing and teasing. Vaughn made it to her first – largely because he tripped Ronan and pushed Seth face first into the cushions on the lounge – picking her up and carting her into the bedroom. She slid down his body, the evidence of his arousal plain to feel. The bulge at the front of his jeans looked big and inviting, and she decided to make him more comfortable by unzipping them carefully and peeling the denim back. His hardness sprang free immediately, long and thick. Looked like someone went commando. She reached out, wrapping her fingers around the solid length, and his moan mingled with her own. He felt wonderful.

Despite her newfound boldness, she couldn't help glancing up to where the camera had been hidden. Vaughn noticed her sudden stillness and the direction of her gaze, and he cupped her face with his hands, redirecting her stare.

"Hey. We found them all. He can't see you, I promise."

She raised her chin, hardening her eyes. "I don't care if you didn't find all the cameras. Fuck him. Let him watch. Let him see how a real man acts."

Vaughn groaned. "Fuck! You're amazing."

He kissed her and kissed her until she began to hallucinate that he had multiple sets of hands, and they were divesting her of her lingerie. Wait, she wasn't imagining anything. There really were extra hands peeling off the lace, caresses and lips trailing in their wake. She fought the urge to giggle like a schoolgirl. She was really doing it. She was soon to have three new lovers in one fell swoop.

Ivory found herself completely naked in no time and passed from man to man as they ripped off their own clothes, flinging them carelessly around the room. She touched and tasted, gasping at the feeling of unyielding muscles under the satin smoothness of tanned skin. The men let her have her fill, as she cupped each of them in turn, learning their shapes and what made them beg. All too soon for her liking, she found her new favourite toys out of reach when they moved away from her and crawled onto the bed. She knew they had been dying to try out the round mattress. She had been aching to see them atop of it as well.

The three of them sprawled on their backs, their hard dicks pointing to the ceiling, as they stroked themselves. She gulped; they looked like demi-gods. No, scrap that. They looked like gods – there was no demi about it.

She sauntered over to the bed until her legs brushed against the mattress. Cupping her breasts, she offered the beaded peaks to the first open mouth she saw: Seth's. Her head fell back on a gasp as his rough tongue stroked over her. She felt hyper-sensitive to his touch, and when strong fingers played over her mound and dipped into her sheath, her knees buckled.

Seth lifted her easily, placing her on top of an already waiting Vaughn. She straddled his waist, flexing her fingers on his chest as he teased her wet entrance with the tip of his broad cock. She shivered in anticipation and moaned in bliss when Seth's hands returned to her breasts from behind, plucking and tugging at her sensitive nipples. Seemed Seth was a boob man. She moved her hips, trying to force Vaughn exactly where she wanted him, but was unable to seat herself.

"Easy, baby. We've got you," Vaughn assured her, sweat already glistening on his forehead. He gave a nod to Seth behind her, and she immediately felt his hands grip her hips, angling them perfectly as Ronan's hand appeared in front of her to grab Vaughn's cock and hold it steady.

"Oh . . ." she murmured breathlessly. The sight of Ronan's tanned, masculine hand against the paler skin of Vaughn's dick made her own sex clench greedily. It had to be the sexiest thing she had ever seen. She couldn't wait to see them making love in front of her. In fact, she desperately hoped Seth and Ronan would do just that while she and Vaughn got it on.

"You like the look of that, huh?" Ronan teased, jacking Vaughn off slowly. Vaughn let out a sharp groan, his hips arching up.

She swallowed audibly, nodding.

"All in good time. For now, this" – he gave Vaughn a firm squeeze – "is all yours." Ronan swooped down, covering her mouth with his own as Seth manoeuvred her hips downward.

Under the guiding hands of her three body-guards, she was slowly and exquisitely filled to her limits. When breathing became a necessity, she pulled away from Ronan, shifting her hips restlessly, aching for Vaughn to move. He grunted at her move-ments and began to pump his hips slowly. She let her head fall back, savouring the sensations cascading throughout her body. Vaughn felt absolutely incredi-ble, but she was hyper-aware that there were two other people in the room as well. Not wanting to leave anybody out, but a little unsure of the mechan-ics, she sought out Seth and Ronan. Seth caught her eye and smiled, walking across the bed on his knees and planting himself conveniently in front of her. And what do you know? If she leaned down just a little, she would be in the perfect position to draw his hardness into her mouth. Although she was more than willing to oblige, she still worried about Ronan.

Seth tangled his fingers in her hair, aiming a smirk beyond her shoulder. "Don't worry about Ro. He likes to watch."

Taking him at his word – he would know – she leaned forwards and engulfed the head of Seth's cock. Three male groans echoed sharply around the room. Seth's hips jack-knifed, pushing his length further down her throat, Vaughn grabbed her hips and began a pounding rhythm, and Ronan's hot breath fanned over her back and neck as he watched the show.

Making love with more than one man at the same time was nothing like she dreamed it would be. It was more – so much more. It was a full on, three-hundred-and-sixty-degree sensory experience. Everywhere she looked, she saw an image of a handsome face twisted in pleasure. The scent of sex and lust hung heavy in the air, and the sounds of groans and flesh against flesh were a symphony of desire. There were six different hands, touching her everywhere at all times, pushing her pleasure higher than she knew was possible. And to top it all off, she had the taste of Seth on her tongue – an erotic mix of earthiness and saltiness.

The rhythm of Seth's hips was becoming erratic, and he was being less careful not to push himself into her willing mouth too deeply. His hands in her hair tugged more roughly and his breath was leaving him in harsh gasps. All in all, she figured his release was imminent. As her own orgasm crept closer and closer with every plunge of Vaughn's hips, she increased the suction of her mouth, flattening her tongue so Seth could slide into her throat. The noise he made was almost like a squeal, and she actually released him to laugh out loud. Seth threw her a disgruntled look before gripping the base of his cock, staving off his orgasm.

"If you can laugh, I'm obviously doing something wrong." Vaughn's voice rumbled over her before he yanked her down, devouring her lips and gripping her butt cheeks hard. She whimpered as her sensitive nipples rubbed against the hair on his chest and held on for dear life when his long plunges turned into short, hard thrusts. The new position had her clit gaining some friction and her orgasm hit her mere seconds later. Crying out loudly, she closed her eyes as bliss, sharp and clear, surged throughout her. The hard body beneath her bucked wildly, a near window-shattering shout resonating from Vaughn's throat as he, too, found his release.

"Quick, baby. Please." The plea came from Ronan. He was next to her head now, the tip of his cock an angry purple and in clear need of its own release. Pushing herself up on one hand, she opened wide, taking him into the warm recess of her mouth. His yell sounded triumphant as he pumped his hips twice, emptying himself while she swallowed convulsively.

Three breathless seconds later, she was lifted and pushed onto her back. Seth came down on top of her, kissing her passionately, even as he palmed her hips. "Ivory?" His face was twisted into a look of tortured need, and yet he still paused, asking permission.

Answering with her actions instead of words, she wrapped her legs around his hips, angling her pelvis to meet his, even as she wrapped her arms around his back, her nails scraping over his flanks. He groaned, taking her up on her offer, plunging into her in one long glide. She gasped as his impressive size dragged through her now highly sensitised folds. The weight of him on top of her and the feel of him inside of her felt different than Vaughn, but just as perfect. Her internal muscles clenched greedily, desperate for more despite the earth-shattering orgasm only minutes before. Seth cupped her hips, pulling out nearly all the way before pushing back in. She arched her neck back, her hands frantically trying to find some purchase now, having slipped from Seth's broad shoulders. Hard hands gripped her own, and she soon found them pinned to the bed above her head. Looking left, she saw a smirking, satisfied Vaughn, and to her right was Ronan, looking a little sleepy but clearly still enjoying the show.

"Ask and ye shall receive," Vaughn whispered naughtily in her ear, obviously referring to her voiced fantasy from earlier.

She was so turned on, she barely had time to process her fantasy come to fruition. Less than a handful of pumps from Seth's hips later, she came in a blinding rush of shivers and gasps and moans. Her head thrashed wildly, and she felt for sure the plea-sure was never going to end. But the hands that firmly held her acted as anchors, making her feel safe instead of out of control. She was dimly aware of Seth reaching his own peak, before she succumbed to the oblivion of sleep.

Seemed they had fulfilled her fantasy in every way.

Fifteen

Ivory woke up alone. She felt the sheets next to her – still warm – and winced a little when hidden muscles protested. So it hadn't been a dream, after all. But where were the men? She struggled to push back the doubt and insecurities that rose to the surface. Was she getting the morning-after brush off? A rush of water and the sound of male voices filtered through the closed en suite door, and she released the breath she was holding. They hadn't left her. They hadn't used her.

Well, not in any way I didn't want to be used, she thought smugly.

Stretching, she reached her hands up high and pushed out her legs, her toes curling in pure indulgence. She felt absolutely frigging fantastic. She had spent the night surrounded by three muscled bodies, being pleasured and pleasuring in return. Whoever had coined the term 'the more the merrier' really knew what they were talking about. She was going to take the morning to bask, not only in the wonderful endorphins pinging through her body, but also in the warm fuzzy feelings bouncing around her heart too.

She didn't think she would ever feel this way about any man, and yet here she was, forming an emotional connection to three at the same time. After last night, she had no doubt she was falling hard and fast for her bodyguards. The thought scared her – there were those secrets of hers that needed to remain hidden. Plus, they were just passing through – not looking to become residents of her small town. She had no real clue as to how to proceed, but just for now, she refused to let those complications take hold. Bask – she was totally going to bask. And what better way to bask than to join the triad of males in their morning shower?

Smiling, she slipped out of bed, unconcerned with her nakedness – no point closing the barn door once the horse had bolted, after all. Pausing with her ear to the door, she could make out the murmur of deep voices, the occasional chuckle . . . and the frequent sound of moans through the aged wood. Looked like the morning playtime was already in full swing. Positively salivating over the thought of three naked, slippery men just inches away, she swung the door open . . . and jerked to a stop, her body going stiff, her breath stilling in her chest. Seth had Ronan pinned to his front in the centre of the bathroom. One of his brawny arms was wrapped around Ronan's magnificent pecs as the other hand gripped his shaft, pumping almost lazily. She could just make out a naked Vaughn in the shower behind them.

But it wasn't the erotic sight that had her heart stuttering in her chest. Ronan's head was thrown back in obvious bliss, his head resting on Seth's broader shoulder. His eyes were closed, but his mouth was slightly open, revealing that some of his teeth had elongated and looked remarkably like fangs . . . or canines. The hand that held him in place also didn't resemble the one from hours earlier, when it had stroked her to completion. The tips of Seth's fingers were now sharp and deadly looking – claws that were idly tracing around Ronan's nipple. His eyes were trained on the motion of his other clawed hand, and they held an eerie glow, the pupils vertical like that of an animal.

She must have made some kind of sound, for

both Ronan and Seth whipped their heads up, glowing eyes focusing on her in a heartbeat. She held both hands in front of her as she backed up a step. "Stay away from me." Her voice sounded thin even to her own ears.

"Ivory!" Seth's shocked voice obviously drew the attention of Vaughn, for he jumped out of the shower in a flash, dripping water everywhere as he took in the scene.

"Who are you? *What* are you?" she demanded, shaking her head. *This couldn't be happening.*

"Ivory . . . it's okay. We can explain." Ronan's voice was low and soothing as he approached her slowly.

"Stop! Don't come any closer!" she yelled. "And stop with your bullshit. I'm not listening to anything you have to say. You're not bodyguards, are you? You're him – my stalker." Her breathing sped up, and she was afraid she was going to hyper-ventilate.

"What?" Seth asked, looking honestly shocked at that. "Why would you think that? Ivory, we would never hurt you. We—"

"Just shut up! God, I can't believe I fell for it. Three sexy men claiming to want me, claiming to feel things they've never felt before? I'm such an idiot. I deserve everything I get." She let out a self-deprecating sound that was half laugh, half sob.

"Honey, just let us explain . . ." Ronan tried again. But she wasn't falling for it. Not ever again.

"No! You're not human. I saw you. You have fangs and claws and your eyes . . . You expect me to believe that's just a coincidence?" she yelled, backing from the room, only to have the three of them mirror her step for step.

"What do you mean, coincidence?" Vaughn's voice was low and held a distinct feline growl.

Ivory shivered as the sound rolled over her naked body, seeming to caress her every curve, stimulating nerves and provoking desires. She was truly losing it here. These men were liars. They had gained her trust, made her believe she was safe with them, only to be the ones who had terrified her in the first place. And on top of all that, she had allowed them to seduce her. While she had been basking in the warm fuzzies, they had no doubt been congratulating themselves on a job well done.

The betrayal nearly felled her. It hurt so much. It was the hurt rather than the anger that had her magic rising up, stripping the powerful glamour away. Her hair grew to her waist, and she watched as the brown locks quickly transformed in colour. Now no longer mousey brown, but a pure snow white and straight as a waterfall, the strands seemed to dance about her body as her power infused the room. She saw the men gasp in shock, their mouths hanging open as they took in the sight of her purple eyes, now sparking with barely contained magic.

She may have been scared of her stalker. She may have needed help. But that was only because she was alone, and she didn't want to reveal herself as the witch she was – not because she was powerless or weak. The permanent glamour she used to alter her features and hide her magic from other witches used a lot of energy. It had taken her months to perfect the spell and then weeks more to wield it. If she'd removed it in order to hunt down her stalker herself, it would have taken months again to manipulate, exposing her and forcing her to move on. But she didn't want to. She loved the little life she had carved out for herself here. But it seemed her plans had been for naught because the very help she had begged for was actually her enemy.

"Holy shit, Ivory!" Seth exclaimed, drawing her attention in his direction. She had never seen a more shell-shocked look on a person's face in all her life.

She smiled, watching as Seth blanched, knowing it wasn't a pleasant smile. "You made a mistake," she informed them, raising her hands and calling on powers, long neglected but never forgotten. The air crackled for a moment, and she flung her hands outward, pushing with her magic. They all grunted, falling back a step . . . but that was it. *What the fuck?* Ivory's gift was telekinesis. She could move all manner of things in all manner of ways. That much power should have had them flying backwards and out through the bathroom wall.

"Why didn't that work? That should have worked," she muttered out loud, glaring at her traitorous hands.

"Your powers won't work on us." Ronan's voice had her raising her hands once again as she concentrated on picking up his body once more.

Nothing. Nada. Zip. Not even a grunt this time. She looked askance at her hands. "Why won't they work?" The question was actually directed at herself once again, but it was Vaughn who answered.

"Because you're our witch."

If she wasn't in such a state of confusion, hurt, and shock, she would have noticed the waver in his strong voice, or the way his hands shook and his eyes watered. But with the realisation that her magic was failing her, came a torrent of panic. "I'm not your anything!" she flung back, racing from the room now in pure terror. Not only were they not human, but they also knew she was a witch. They had to be the ones terrorising her. There was no other explanation.

"Ivory, wait!" Shouts and heavy footsteps followed her, spurring her on and intensifying her fear. Drawing on her only remaining weapon, she called up her animal. The beast was her biggest and most harboured secret – even more so than the fact she could wield magic. It answered in a heartbeat, a furious yowl sounding in her head. Warmth spread through her body, nerve endings coming to life as white fur sprouted from her skin. She felt her bones elongate and hands turn to paws as she lowered to all fours on the ground. Her senses heightened and her predator instincts sharpened exponentially.

Trapped. The animal growled, seeing no escape through the closed doors and windows. Sound behind her had her arching her back and hissing furiously as three men stopped and stared. *Never seen a jungle cat in a lounge room before?* Ivory thought sarcastically, some of her confidence returning now that she was merged with her inner beast. Not that it was *her* feelings – not at all. Her cat was a cocky little bitch.

"What. The. Fuck?"

Ivory flicked her tail sharply at the astonishment in Seth's voice. She may be trapped – probably should have opened the door while she still had opposable thumbs – and her telekinesis may be on the fritz, but she was by no means vulnerable. She planned to teach these boys what happened when you cornered a cat. They would rue the day they ever thought they could stalk and seduce a white witch.

Sixteen

"**W**hat. The. Fuck?"

Seth's incredulous voice gained Vaughn's attention, but he didn't dare take his eyes off the animal in the corner of the room. Not only would it be incredibly dumb and dangerous, but he couldn't have forced his eyes away even if he tried. Their witch. Ivory was their witch. Somehow, someway, Ivory was a witch of the Panthera bloodline. It shouldn't have been possible for so many reasons. Not the least was that he had truly given up hope of ever finding a witch remaining from his coven.

Two and a half lifetimes he had lived, a familiar with no witch, and no end in sight to his lack of purpose. He knew Seth had always believed, but he, and even Ronan, had just been going through the motions these last few years.

On top of that, he should have recognised Ivory's magic the moment she was in his presence – they all should have. He had watched the transformation from average, plain Jane, to exquisite feminine beauty and knew she must have been using a glamour to change her appearance. But it shouldn't have affected their ability to sense her magic. And it sure as shit shouldn't have affected their ability to sense she had an inner animal. Their panthers should have been foaming at the mouth over her. It must have been one hell of a powerful glamour.

"Are you all seeing what I'm seeing?" Seth spoke again.

"Are you seeing a white panther with purple eyes promising our death next to the television?" Ronan asked, sounding far too mild in Vaughn's opinion.

Seth's head bobbled as he nodded. "Uh huh."

"Then yep. I'm seeing what you're seeing."

"How is this possible?" Seth asked.

"She's a witch from the Panthera bloodline," Vaughn stated, more so he could hear the words out loud rather than in answer to Seth's question.

Seth swiped a hand through the air. "Not that. That's obvious. My body recognises her magic in every single pore." Seth threw a triumphant and cocky grin in his direction – the little shit. "Meaning I was right, by the way. I'm talking about the fact that she's a shapeshifter. I thought only familiars could do that."

The shapeshifter in question pinned her ears back and hissed at them again, long white tail swishing in clear agitation. Seemed she didn't like being spoken about like she wasn't there. Well, if she would change back and listen to reason, they could get everything sorted out. Surely she must be able to feel the connection now too. The recognition of a witch and their familiar went both ways. "Ivory, shift back now so we can talk," he stated, being practical.

A deep rumble in the feline chest was his only answer, and he took a step forwards, lacking patience. He wanted answers, dammit. A large paw with claws unsheathed flashed out, quick as lightening, and had him cursing up a storm. He grabbed his forearm as blood began dripping in a steady stream onto the hardwood floor.

"Dammit, Vaughn!" Ronan yelled, rushing to him and covering the deep gashes with his own hand.

"Will you show some common sense, please? She's terrified. I don't know what the hell is going on here, but you should know better than to pressure a predator."

"Fuck," he gritted out. He did know better, but he was so damn befuddled right now. Disbelief was warring with hope, and it was making him testy. "How would you like to proceed, oh wise one?" His voice was laced with sarcasm – his automatic defence mechanism – and he saw Ronan's eyes narrow dangerously. So, Ronan wasn't as unaffected by everything as he appeared. The knowledge had him relaxing his stance a bit and taking a deep breath.

"Don't be an arse," Ronan snapped back.

"Can't seem to help it," he admitted.

"Don't I know it," Ronan muttered. "We need to proceed with caution."

"Be my guest." He gestured to the hissing, spitting creature in the corner.

Ronan glared at him once more before lifting his hand off the scratches. The bleeding had slowed and they were already healing. Familiars healed fast. It was one of the perks of sharing your spirit with an animal. "Just let me think a minute," his lover groused, clearly displeased with the whole situation.

"We need to talk to her cat."

Vaughn startled a little as he and Ronan spun to face Seth, who was eyeing the beautiful white creature with appreciation. "What?"

"We need to talk to her animal," he repeated. "Our panthers are all instinct, right? It's us humans who are all logic. So, it's her human half that's fighting us. We have our own panthers – have you bothered to listen to what yours is telling you?" Seth asked, crossing his arms over his naked chest.

"What the hell are you talking about, Seth?" Vaughn was not in the mood for Seth's stupid antics.

Seth rolled his eyes but walked over to him. He unsheathed a claw and ran it down the centre of Vaughn's chest, purring at the same time. Vaughn's panther never failed to react to one of the members in its shadow. Not only did he always recognise the panthers as fellow familiars, but Vaughn's panther thought of them as mates. Despite the tense situation, his furry spirit reacted predictably to Seth's seductive feline and rose up, scenting its male mates. But to Vaughn's shock, it also scented another mate – one that could breed. His jaw fell open, disbelieving eyes darting to the white panther.

"You feel it now?" Seth asked, stroking a soothing hand down his uninjured arm.

He could only nod mutely.

"Feel what?" Ronan demanded, obviously still very much in human mode.

"She's our mate."

Seventeen

" S he's our mate," Seth stated.

He watched as Ronan also took a deep breath, his eyes widening comically. "How is this possible?" he asked.

Seth shrugged. He had no idea. He was the fresh soul here. They were the ones who had been around the block a few times. If anyone knew what the hell was going on, it should be one of them. Besides, quite frankly, he didn't really care. All he cared about was soothing the female panther just metres away.

"Well, what do we do now?" Ronan asked, still looking completely bewildered.

Seth shrugged again. Why were they asking him? "What do you *want* to do?" he offered.

"Honestly? I want to pin her to the ground, mount her, and sink my teeth into her."

Ronan's words had his dick springing back to life in a nanosecond, and a quick look revealed the same impact on Vaughn. They were all still standing around naked, not having taken the time to throw on clothes when Ivory had bolted.

Growling echoed throughout the room, and Seth saw Ronan's words were not taken in quite the same way by the white panther. In fact, she had hunched down low, her shoulders bunching as if ready to pounce. And if he wasn't mistaken, her eerily pretty violet eyes were trained intensely on the hard evidence of their desire. Quickly shielding his now deflated manhood with one cupped hand, he held his other up in surrender – or supplication.

"Probably not the wisest course of action at the moment, Ronan," he spoke from the corner of his mouth, never taking his eyes from Ivory.

"Understatement of the year," Vaughn commented, pushing Ronan in front of him as a human shield.

Ronan threw his partner a disgusted look at the cowardly, albeit smart, move. "How do we fix this?"

Seth didn't think he had ever seen Ro looking so lost before. The man always had all the answers.

Looking to his other lover, he found him in a similar state of confusion and unease. And they treated *him* like a child more often than not?! Their reactions were understandable though, he guessed. They had served their coven faithfully for generations, and he knew they had both given up hope of finding any remaining members. This had to be a huge shock to their systems. On top of that, Ivory did indeed smell like a mate. As far as Seth knew, such a thing was unheard of.

Sure, both Vaughn and Ronan smelled like mates to him. But that was due to the fact they had been lovers for years and their animals had claimed each other as surely as their human halves had. Although a physical and mental attraction had been there from the moment he had met her, he had yet to form that same solid, intimate bond with Ivory. However, his panther was practically grinding its teeth in agitation to get to what it considered its female, suggesting Ivory was their natural life-mate.

Figuring his two companions were going to be fairly useless – Vaughn had no patience and Ronan was spouting words like 'mount' – Seth determined he was going to have to talk the female off the ledge. Taking a deep breath, he relaxed his muscles as much as possible, coaxing his panther to the forefront of his mind. It wasn't exactly difficult – the creature really did want to get to its mate. His transformation took mere seconds, then he was staring down at fur and paws instead of skin and hands. He immediately opened his mouth, scenting the air, whiskers twitching as the delicious aroma of female assaulted senses which were far more sensitive now in this form.

Cautioning himself and his other half to take it easy, he remained low as he slowly crept across the space keeping them apart. Ivory still held herself tense, and there was still a resounding rumble deep in her throat, but he could see her nose twitching. Her mouth opened a moment later, and he knew she was scenting him as he had her. He only hoped he smelled as good to her cat as hers did to him.

When he was only about one metre away, he lowered himself to the floor and immediately rolled to his back, exposing his vulnerable, soft belly. The female cocked her head to the side, looking curious despite herself, and Seth batted a sheathed claw playfully in the air. He heard Vaughn snort derisively at his antics – no doubt storing this away for future humiliation – but Seth didn't care. His primary goal right now was to look as non-threatening as possible. It was kind of a hard task, considering his panther was almost twice the size of her more feminine form. He allowed a purr to rumble in his chest as he relaxed his head onto the floor, green eyes beseeching purple ones.

Seconds ticked by agonizingly slowly, but eventually the white cat closed the distance between them. She lowered her head towards him tentatively, nose twitching and eyes roaming as she took in his form. One more step and she was within touching distance. Seth cautioned his animal not to move, knowing Ivory needed him to be the submissive in this scenario. She walked in a slow circle around him, sniffing every part of his body, before finally pushing her furred face against his neck almost affectionately. She continued to rub her cheek over his face and neck, and he knew he would now be covered in her scent. Their scent glands were located in their cheeks, and it was how they marked their territory. His panther began purring, satisfied that the female considered him hers. As for Seth, his heart began thumping in relief and triumph. She recognised them now. She had to.

Hoping she was comfortable enough, he shifted back to his human form, remaining seated on the floor. Ivory didn't flinch away from him, but she didn't shift back either. He decided to give her a bit more time and took the opportunity of being so close to study her. She was definitely a jaguar like them, but she wasn't pure white – not like he and the others were pure black. Her undercoat was white, and her spots were a very pale grey. In the wild, such markings were extremely rare, he knew. But not rare enough they didn't have a name – ghost jaguars. He had never seen a ghost jaguar – or white panther – shifter before. She was beautiful. Raising his hand, he was pleased when the animal allowed him to stroke the softness of her head. She purred, bumping her head against his hand and he smiled.

"You're a very pretty jaguar, Ivory. Won't you shift back now? We would never hurt you, I promise. Can't you feel what your cat is feeling? Trust it. Trust us. Shift back for us so we can talk," he crooned, stroking in long motions.

A shimmering displacement in the air accompanied her shift, and soon enough, a gloriously naked Ivory crouched in front of him. The dips and curves of the body were familiar, but the face was not. This face held higher, sharper cheekbones, fuller lips, a pointier chin, and a straighter nose. Her eyes were a wild and unearthly shade of violet, and her hair, once brown and shoulder length, was now pure white and kissing the curve of her bottom.

She was stunningly, outrageously beautiful.

His hand rose of its own accord, wanting nothing more than to touch and discover this new Ivory – the woman who was not only a witch from his coven but somehow also his mate. But apparently, she was still skittish and not willing to trust yet. She scrambled back on all fours before climbing gracefully to her feet. She raised her hands, palms out, as if preparing them as weapons.

"There's no need for that, Ivory. We won't hurt you – you must know that. Just as you must know by now that your magic won't work on us." Vaughn's voice was gruff from emotion, Seth knew. But the bluntness of his words, coupled with the rasp in his voice, made him sound harsh. Ivory obviously thought so too because she flicked her hand in the direction of the heavy antique lamp in the corner of the room. Seth watched as it floated easily in the air.

"My magic may not work on you directly, but I'm betting this lamp sure will." She cocked an eyebrow that was a shade darker than the hair on her head.

"We need you—" Vaughn began.

"Don't! Don't tell me what *you* need. *I* need you to tell me what the hell is going on here. Who are you? Where are you from? Why are you here?" She pelted them with questions and Seth could feel her anxiety levels rising once more. "Why does my magic recognise you? Why does my jaguar want you?"

"We'll explain everything," Ronan's deep voice soothed. "But maybe we should all get dressed first, hmm?"

Ivory startled at that, amethyst eyes darting around the room before glancing at her own naked body, and she blushed prettily. Her pale skin pinked easily, and Seth couldn't help wanting to see how rosy this new version of Ivory became in the heat of passion. She gestured with her hand and a heartbeat later, the fluffy robe from the back of the lounge was within her grasp. She shrugged it on quickly and tied the sash. Their little witch certainly had a handy primary power. He couldn't wait to see what else she could do.

Eighteen

R onan lectured himself sternly to not keep staring at the woman in front of him. A witch. Ivory was a witch. And not just any witch. She was a witch from the Panthera bloodline, the coven he had been serving for generations. The same coven they had been searching endlessly for over the years. And what's more, she was a white panther – which should have been impossible. Witches didn't shapeshift.

"Stop staring," Ivory muttered, shifting uncomfortably.

"I can't help it. Ivory, you are . . ." he couldn't finish the sentence, unable to find the words to describe how utterly gorgeous she was. He had thought her quiet beauty absolutely stunning this past week, cursing himself numerous times for initially thinking of her as plain when he had first met her. The more he got to know her, the more her beauty came to the surface. He had grown to love looking into her chocolate eyes, their warmth shining brightly above the dusting of freckles on her nose. Her brown hair had always been lustrous and soft, and every time she moved, he could smell vanilla, rain, and earth. But this Ivory . . . this Ivory was otherworldly. It was taking all his control not to reach out and touch the pale perfection of her hair to see if it was as silky as it looked. Her eyes glowed like luminous gems of amethyst. And the visions that filled his head at those pouty lips of hers . . .

"Ronan!"

"Huh?" He jerked, seeing the amused smirks on the faces of his male lovers, and the exasperation on Ivory's. He must have been staring at her like some kind of daft, sex-crazed lunatic for the past couple of minutes. "Sorry," he muttered, commanding himself not to blush.

Ivory cleared her throat, squirming under their collective gazes. "Just stop staring and start talking."

"Where do you want us to start?" he asked – there, see? He could articulate.

She huffed out an annoyed breath. "How about

the part where you just happen to be familiars, and I just happen to be a witch—and I just happen to have a stalker and you just happen to be bodyguards for hire!" Ivory began speaking softly and slowly, but by the end of her tirade she was yelling and speaking so fast he could barely keep up with her. She panted, out of breath from her one long sentence.

"You know about familiars?" Seth asked, sounding surprised.

Ronan couldn't blame him. Ivory's shocked and terrified reaction had him assuming she was somehow ignorant of their origins.

She eyed them all drolly. "I'm a witch. Of course I know what familiars are. That isn't what I want to know. I want to know what you're doing here."

"Protecting you," Vaughn pointed out. "What you hired us to do."

She snorted rudely. "Bullshit! You really expect me to believe you had no idea I was a witch? That this is just some kind of insane coincidence? Coincidences are for morons." She levelled her purple peepers at them. "And I'm no moron."

Vaughn laughed, but there was no humour in the sound. "Trust me, I'm not into coincidences either. Maybe you're setting us up, hmm? Trying to catch yourself a familiar or two?"

Ivory sneered at him. "Why in the world would I want to catch a familiar? I've never been near one in my whole life."

"Never? Why is that, exactly?" Ronan asked, keeping his voice mildly curious rather than the antagonistic tone of Vaughn's. The man was practically drowning in his terrified hope, and it was making him defensive. Still, pushing Ivory was unlikely to get him the answers he desired. "Witches and familiars kind of go hand in hand."

She shifted her gaze to him, narrowing her eyes in suspicion. "Don't try that good 'ol country boy tone with me, Ronan. It won't work. You lied to me – have been lying to me since the day we met."

"*We* lied to *you*? Hypocrite much?" Vaughn snorted, running agitated fingers through his already dishevelled hair. "Your whole face was a lie!"

Ronan cringed at Vaughn's tone – both accusatory and laced with hurt. He really wished he would stop with the bad attitude, but it was his go-to mode whenever he was feeling vulnerable. Besides, Ronan could actually understand the hurt. He had been slowly and surely falling for the brunette barkeeper, and the others had been as well. To suddenly realise the face of the person they had spent the night making love with wasn't even real . . . he shook his head. Yeah, hurt was the right word.

Ivory remained silent, not responding to Vaughn's words. She had lost some of the stiffness in her shoulders, but her face was still wary.

"Ivory, talk to us. Obviously we've stumbled onto something a little more complicated than an average stalker case. You and Vaughn may not be fans of coincidences, but I sure am. Anything that brought us to you is fine by me." Seth grinned, open and eager, and Ronan saw Ivory relax just a little bit more.

Thank heavens for Seth, he thought.

"You're all really bodyguards? You aren't my stalker? Or witch hunters? This is just some random twist of fate?" she asked, her wariness mixed with what he thought was hope.

"Ivory, I promise you – none of us are your stalker. And we sure aren't hunters. We would never do anything to harm you. In fact, our whole purpose in life is to keep you safe – to keep you happy and healthy and cared for," Seth rushed to assure her.

She seemed to be listening now at least, although the frown remained firmly in place. "What are you talking about? I know you are bodyguards, but that seems a little excessive."

"Well . . ." Seth elongated the word, looking at him and Vaughn for guidance. Vaughn simply shrugged. As for himself, he motioned for Seth to keep going. Ivory was responding—that was all that mattered for now. "How much do you know about witches and familiars?" he asked.

Ivory looked wary again but answered, "Only what my mother told me: familiars are like guides and companions to their witches."

"She's right, we are that, but also so much more," Ronan confirmed. "Where is she now?"

"She died twelve years ago." Ivory looked towards Vaughn. "I didn't lie about not having any family. I've been on my own since I was eighteen."

Vaughn's green eyes had lost their defensive spark, and he was now leaning forwards out of interest rather than anger. "I'm sorry, Ivory. I don't think you're a liar. This is all just a shock."

She laughed at that, the sound blessedly familiar. "You're telling me! I can hardly believe this. And you don't want to hurt me?" she asked again.

They looked at each other in confusion. Other than the fact that they had told her numerous times they would never hurt her, Ivory had just described familiars to them. Surely she understood it was practically impossible for familiars to harm a witch

– let alone a witch in their own coven. "Ivory, familiars don't harm witches. We serve them." He made sure his voice was no nonsense, leaving no room for her uncertainty.

She lowered her head, fingers twisting nervously in her robe. "But I'm not just a witch, am I?"

No, she most definitely was not just a witch. It was an oddity, and one he was yearning to learn more about, but it didn't change the fact that she was still a witch from the Panthera Coven.

"Yeah, we kinda noticed." Seth chuckled. "You're a ghost jaguar – a white panther. It may not be normal to most, but we're hardly in a position to judge given we shapeshift into black jaguars – or panthers, if you prefer to call us that."

She looked up quickly, eyeing them all individually. "You're all panthers?"

They nodded, with Vaughn adding a "Yep."

"Is that why my cat likes you so much? Because we're all the same species?" she queried.

"Your cat likes us?" The question came from Vaughn.

She nodded. "She wants to roll around in your scent. It's weird."

Ronan wanted to shout with joy. Ivory felt the mate pull – well, her cat did anyway. She didn't seem to understand what it was, though, and Ronan knew they had to tread carefully. They were making progress – Ivory no longer looked like she wanted to bolt – but there were still so many unanswered questions on both sides.

"My panther likes your scent too," Ronan assured her. And then it struck him. No wonder she smelled like all three of them! Her panther belonged to their panthers, which meant she also belonged to them. But why hadn't his feline friend been clawing at him, trying to get to its mate this entire time? Sure, the instant attraction had been there. But it was nothing like the urge to claim her now. He looked at Seth and Vaughn, and saw that they were also breathing in, nostrils flaring, shifting uncomfortably. They were definitely noticing the increased intensity of Ivory's scent.

"That glamour of yours must have been super powerful," Seth pointed out, arriving at the same conclusion Ronan was about to. "My panther didn't recognise yours, let alone any of us recognising your magical bloodline."

Ivory nodded, twirling a strand of hair around her finger and drawing all their riveted gazes. "It was. It altered my appearance but also completely dampened my magic, as well as my cat. That was the whole point of it – to hide."

"But not from your stalker? You've had the glamour in place longer than that," Vaughn stated.

She chewed on her lip, hesitating, and Ronan bit back his frustration. She still didn't trust them.

"I'm sorry. I'm not trying to be difficult." Her voice was small as she looked at him, clearly picking up on his thoughts.

He sighed. Now he was the one acting like a dick. "It's okay, sweetheart. I'm sorry too. It's been a day full of surprises for everyone. I assume your stalker and the fact that you've been using a glamour to hide are two different issues?"

She snorted. "Seems that way."

"We can't do much about the stalker at the moment, so why don't you tell us what you've been hiding from? Is it hunters?" That was the most logical explanation. "And why do you keep asking us if we're going to hurt you?"

Nineteen

V aughn stood and walked over to the lounge Ivory was seated on. He made sure to keep his movements slow and non-threatening, not wanting to scare her or get her panther's back up again. Now that she wasn't poised to knock him on the head with a lamp or run away from them screaming, he was able to control his cat's dominant nature more.

He knew he had been acting like a jerk before, but he couldn't help it. His panther believed Ivory was theirs and was prowling restlessly in his mind now that he could scent Ivory's own jaguar. His beast was demanding she acknowledge him – all of them. He needed to be close to her. He seated himself next to her but not within touching distance, receiving a small smile. He released a pent-up breath – so far so good.

"What he said." He angled his head in Ronan's direction, referring to his lover's earlier questions.

She looked deeply into his eyes for a moment, and although hers were an entirely different colour now, he could still see his Ivory in them. He stilled. *His Ivory?* Sure, his panther was very vocal about the whole 'mate' thing, but Vaughn was also still a man. When had he started thinking of her as his?

The feeling had probably been creeping up on him for days now and culminated last night when they had made love with her. And that is exactly what it had been – not sex, but lovemaking. It was a wholly unexpected but not unwanted or unpleasant realisation, he acknowledged. They hadn't been able to bask in the morning-after endorphins or analyse what the evening of pleasure had meant to them all, but he was fairly certain his men were on the same page. He only hoped what Ivory was about to reveal didn't change his blossoming feelings. There was still a part of him that was suspicious.

"You can trust us," Seth prompted, when the silence stretched out.

Ivory drew in a deep breath and nodded her head. "My cat seems to think I can. And I . . . I think so too. So, okay then. No, I'm not hiding from witch hunters. Mum cautioned me about them, but I've never seen a single one. I used the glamour so nobody would know I was a witch. I'm hiding from the conclave."

Vaughn was shocked. "You're hiding from the conclave? What the hell for?"

The conclave was what they called their witching governing body. It was made up of one member from each of the twelve ruling covens – well, eleven covens now because the Panthera Coven was believed to be extinct at worst – or lost at best. The conclave made laws, kept the peace, settled disputes, and anything else a normal government would do. They were sometimes annoying, and Vaughn didn't always agree with every decision they made, but that was politicians for you.

"Because of what I am . . . half familiar," Ivory let her bombshell fall into the stunned silence of the room.

"Half familiar?" Seth asked.

"Half fucking familiar?" Vaughn asked.

"You're half familiar. Of course you are. That explains a lot," was Ronan's mild response. Vaughn could have punched him. He was always so cool – outwardly anyway.

"Well, technically, I'm a quarter familiar. My father was human. My mother was a witch and her father was a witch, but her mother was a familiar. Mum could shift too, and at first she wasn't sure I would be able to because of my human blood. But the ability to shapeshift doesn't seem to be diluted through the generations. My panther is strong," Ivory explained in a bit of a rush. It was as if now that she'd started sharing, she wanted to get it all out at once.

"Okay. This explains why you have a panther, but not why you're hiding," Vaughn pointed out. It was extremely rare for a witch and a familiar to have children. It was quite common for them to be lovers, but a witch tended to marry and have children with other witches. Although he'd heard of cases of mixed-breed children, he had never met any.

Ivory looked at him as if it was obvious. "Because I'm not a pureblood. When my grandfather found out his familiar was pregnant with his child, he was threatened by the conclave. They were going to force him to get rid of the baby – they weren't going to suffer a half-breed in the coven's bloodline. He refused, running away and hiding with my grandmother. She died when my mother was very young, as did my grandfather. But they both instilled the importance of staying hidden from the conclave. They said she would be killed if they found her. She told me the same. We spent our whole lives trying to stay hidden. And then when she died, and I ventured out on my own, I knew I needed something more permanent to conceal me. That's when I used the powerful glamour spell."

Vaughn looked at Ronan and then Seth. Seth merely shrugged, not having had much to do with the conclave given he had been born into a generation with a missing bloodline. Ronan, on the other hand, looked just as confused as he was, if his frown was anything to go by.

"Ivory," Ronan began slowly, "that doesn't sound . . . accurate."

Ivory sat up straight. "I assure you it is. Do you really think my grandfather would have taken my grandmother and hidden in the damn wilderness if they weren't in danger? Or maybe you just think my mother lied to me all my life?" Ivory was getting testy again.

Ronan held up his hands. "I'm not saying that. I just think there may have been some kind of misunderstanding."

"Say, Ivory, what was your grandfather's name?"

Seth hurriedly jumped in, clearly seeing the displeasure on Ivory's flawless new face.

She pursed her lips, but answered, "Dale Anthera."

Vaughn jolted hard, jumping up. "That's not possible! Dale was killed in an accident with the only female familiar in our coven more than . . ." He trailed off, realisation striking him like a lightning bolt. "He faked his own death?"

Ivory was already nodding. "He didn't have a choice. He loved her and the baby. He wasn't going to allow them to be hurt."

Vaughn paced across the room. He and Ronan had been familiars to Dale, along with Maree. With only the three of them left, and Dale the only remaining witch in the Panthera Coven, they had shared the duties. He knew the two were lovers but had vastly underestimated their relationship, it would seem. He harboured heavy feelings of guilt for countless years over the death of his charge, had spiralled into a depressed, semi-alcoholic arsehole for almost an entire lifetime, then been pretty much a dick in the one-and-a-half lifetimes since. All because he believed in his own futility; it was useless to be a familiar if you had no witch. But there had

been one, Dale . . . then another, Ivory's mother . . .
and now Ivory.

Sensing his turmoil, Ivory stood and walked over
to him, placing a gentle hand on his tense arm. "You
knew him."

He gritted his teeth, afraid to speak in case he
was rude again – it wasn't her fault. She hadn't even
been born yet. But shooting the messenger was
always an easy thing to do.

Luckily, Ronan spoke up. "Yes. We knew him. He
was our witch, along with Maree. He died under our
watch – at least, we thought he did. We believed he
was the last surviving witch in the Panthera bloodline. When he was killed, times were . . . *difficult*," he
murmured. Talk about the understatement of the
century.

"I'm sorry." Ivory continued to stroke Vaughn's
arm, and he grabbed her hand, grateful for the comfort
and contact. She continued, "He truly believed there
was no other choice; he was in fear for his child's life."

"I believe *you* believe that. But I still don't think
it's right. The conclave doesn't go around killing
babies." He couldn't fathom why Dale would even
think such a thing.

Ivory frowned and removed her hand. His

panther snarled in his mind, wanting her touch back. "I can't tell you anything else. As I said, he was dead before I was even born. I'm just repeating what my mother told me."

"We'll go to the conclave – get this all sorted out." Ronan's voice was low and probably supposed to be soothing.

"What? No!" Ivory's face contorted in fear. "Have you not been listening? I'm part familiar, part witch. They'll kill me!"

Seth jumped up and wrapped his big arms around her. She allowed it but remained stiff. "We would never let them hurt you. Besides, I think Ronan and Vaughn are right. Something doesn't add up. Maybe there was some kind of miscommunication or something."

She snorted. "Pretty fucking big miscommunication."

"It would be, yes," Ronan agreed. "Give us some time to ponder this and look into it. If the time comes we feel we need to go to the conclave directly, we'll discuss it with you first. I promise."

Ronan was such a good little diplomat, Vaughn thought. It was one of the reasons he always liked dirtying the man up. Looking at Ivory, he could see the indecision warring on her face. He couldn't reconcile her fear of the conclave with his own experiences, but he couldn't argue that it was genuine on her end. Trusting them with her biggest secret must be incredibly difficult for her. She was chewing on those fuller, poutier lips of hers and Vaughn wanted to be finished with the talking and get back to the screwing. He didn't think that was likely to be happening anytime soon, and he let out a deflated sigh.

Ivory glanced at him, then Ronan, and looked up at Seth before finally stepping out of his arms. "You're all familiars charged with serving my bloodline, aren't you? If you were my grandfather's familiars, then you must be . . . mine . . . right?"

Seth smiled. "That's right. Ivory, you can't possibly understand what kind of a miracle you are. Everyone believes the Panthera bloodline is extinct. But here you are."

"Here I am," she repeated dully. "I guess that explains why I felt an immediate attraction to all of you. With my glamour down, it's so obvious that my magic recognises you. But I suppose I must have felt it on a subconscious level."

"That's not why. Don't reduce our attraction to magic. It's natural – couldn't be more natural. You're our mate." Vaughn was quick to defend the intimacy of their attraction.

"I'm your what now?" she looked startled – and not altogether pleased.

"Mate," he spat out again. "It means—"

"I know what a mate is – I watch *Animal Kingdom*." Her pissy tone was a match for his. "Your panthers think I'm their mate?" she questioned again, eyeing them all warily.

"Mine doesn't just think it – he knows it. Listen to your animal, what's it telling you?" Vaughn urged, trying to rein in his impatience.

Ivory tilted her head, her hair shimmering like water in the light as it fell over her shoulder. She extended a claw on her pointer finger, tapping it against her knee. "Right now, mine is telling me to slice your balls off for acting like a jerk."

The confrontational tone had Vaughn's pupils slitting vertically for a second as a lecherous grin tilted his lips. Vaughn's cat thrived on confrontation – it was all foreplay to him.

"Ivory, our panthers noticed your unique scent when we first met you; it's a combination of all three of us. Fresh earth, thunderstorms, and vanilla. With your glamour dulling your magic and your animal, it was the only clue we noticed. But we must have recognised it on some level. I mean, it explains why we are all so outrageously captivated with each other," Ronan elaborated in a reasonable tone.

But it seemed Ivory wasn't interested in being reasonable, if her narrowed eyes and stubborn jawline were anything to go by. "You're saying the only reason we're attracted to each other is because of some ridiculous animal instinct? Don't you see how insulting that is?"

"What? No, I mean yes . . . sort of," Ronan blabbered, shaking his head. "Why is it insulting?"

"You're kidding, right? You basically just admitted you were acting on some primal predisposition rather than any kind of actual like for me. If our panthers didn't want each other, you wouldn't have even looked twice at me."

"Well, our panthers do want you. You're our mate. That makes us yours." Vaughn felt the childish urge to poke out his tongue and say, "So there!"

"Well, maybe I don't want you to be mine." Ivory crossed her arms over her chest, causing her breasts to plump and reveal a tantalising view of her cleavage. His cat purred in the back of his mind. Damn cat didn't know what was good for it. They were getting an arse-chewing from the woman and the stupid beast was still purring in ecstasy.

"That's not what you said last night," he threw back, with no small amount of smugness.

Ivory narrowed her eyes dangerously once again, and Ronan shook his head. "Vaughn . . . really not helping, brother."

"Ivory. That's enough now. You're being difficult, twisting our words, and turning something miraculous into something cheap." Seth's voice was low and stern – not something the happy-go-lucky man usually projected. He was losing his patience as well. "The fact that someone on this planet is your perfect match chemically, emotionally, spiritually – and everything in between – is a blessing. It's not a curse. How many people do you think are given such a gift?"

Ivory opened and closed her mouth a couple of times, before slumping back and covering her face with her hands. "You're right. I'm being a total bitch." She peeked between her fingers, violet irises shining bright. "I'm sorry. I just . . ."

"It's okay. I think all our nerves are fried." Seth rubbed her knee.

She dropped her hands, sighing and offering a weak smile. "Yeah. I'm going to go get dressed and then head downstairs for a while – alone."

"What? Ivory, we—"

"Please, just give me some space. I need to think – to process." Her eyes beseeched him to understand.

He looked to the others, knowing he didn't want her out of his sight for a second but also knowing that some time apart was probably a good thing. Tensions were high and everyone was getting frustrated. Better to have a time-out before anyone said or did anything they would regret. "Fair enough. But you can't go anywhere alone, remember? Nothing has changed. Someone still has their sights set on you," he reminded her.

"I know. I'm not going to do anything stupid. I'll just go down to the bar – work on something mindless, like the inventory. I promise."

She ran a hand through her hair, the satiny strands catching the light and giving them an almost silver glow. He was completely entranced by the movement, but it also brought the issue of her appearance to the forefront. "There's one other thing – your glamour. Can you redo it? Otherwise, your employees are going to get a bit of a shock."

She looked positively startled as she glanced in the mirror hanging on the wall. He saw her touch her face, a sad look entering her eyes for a moment before she squared her shoulders. "I can't do the exact same one. It was semi-permanent, only dispersing when I willed it to – something I never had any intention of doing. When I decided to settle here, it took me months and months to perfect that spell and store up enough power to make it work. Until then, I had been doing daily glamours. I guess I'll have to go back to doing that."

With that, she closed her eyes and ran her hands over her hair. White strands made way for brown, freckles once again marred porcelain skin, and exotic eyes became ordinary brown. He tried very hard not to tell her to change back immediately. Now that he had seen the real Ivory, he found this one almost distasteful.

It wasn't her appearance – he would find her beautiful no matter what guise she wore. But it was the fact she seemed to lose some of her spark when the glamour was in place. One day soon they would find answers to her strange past and a solution to hiding her face. But at the moment, the most pressing issue was the sick fuck threatening her. Nothing mattered more than her safety – even their own happiness.

Twenty

I vory fled downstairs and into the sanctuary of her cellar. The room was dark and cool, chilling her heated cheeks and calming her wildly beating heart. The dim and the quiet were exactly what she needed to gather her scrambling thoughts.

Familiars? Mates? She shook her head, remembering when the most stressful part of her day was waking up to a dead bunny on her doorstep. What was she supposed to do with three domineering men who were connected to her magically? And what was worse, they believed she was also connected to them on a primal level.

She plonked her butt down on the nearest box, telling her cat to shut the hell up. The darn thing had been mewling and purring ever since Seth had shifted in front of her. It had no doubt whatsoever that Seth and the other two male black jaguars were meant for her.

Stupid horny cat! she groused. Now that the more powerful glamour had dissolved, she easily recognised them as familiars – her familiars. Her mother had told her all about familiars and witches, so she knew there was a natural magical bond between familiars and their covens. Having never been exposed to such relationships, she never felt she was lacking anything. But now that her magic was reaching out to the three familiars, she realised there was a big empty space where her magic resided. She found herself wanting to ask them to do things for her, or just be with her – in a completely non-sexual way. It was like she wanted them to be her best friends or something. It was very odd but felt so natural at the same time.

However, the second her panther chimed in on the situation, it was all about the sexual feelings. Her cat did indeed love the smell of the three men. Even with the glamour in place, she had to fight the animal's desire to shift and run back upstairs. But the human part of her had meant what she said to Vaughn; was their attraction, their intimacy, nothing more than animal instinct coupled with a bloodline bond? The thought hurt her more than it should have. She didn't want to be reduced to fate – no matter how cool that was. She wanted to be a choice.

She sighed, kicking her feet against her makeshift chair and hearing a dull thud. Looking down, she discovered she was sitting on a box that held two dozen bottles of a truly lovely white wine. Taking it as a sign from the alcohol gods, she had the box opened and the cork popped in one minute flat. She tipped the bottle back and did a decent job of being a frat boy – skulling a third of the contents in one breath.

"Whoa, Ivory?!"

The deep voice behind her interrupted her concentration from her wine guzzling and she choked, inhaling the bubbles instead of swallowing them. A hard hand patted and rubbed her on the back until she was able to stand upright and breathe again.

"Lee?" she coughed out.

"Yeah. What the hell are you doing?" He was eyeing her as if she was some kind of closet alcoholic or something.

"I was just, um, testing the wine," she stuttered, ingeniously holding it up to the light spilling through the now open cellar door. "It has a smooth, easy finish, with ripe, tropical fruit flavours and a hint of gooseberry." She nodded her head sagely. "Great depth of flavours."

He didn't look convinced. "This isn't a regular occurrence, is it?"

She lowered the bottle and rolled her eyes. "No, Lee. I don't make a habit of hiding in the dark and swilling our wine supplies. What are you doing here anyway?" she asked, changing the subject.

"It's almost ten. Libby and I are on the early shift today. You're not supposed to be in until three," he informed her.

Almost ten? It was later than she thought. The bar opened at eleven, but whoever was on first shift arrived about an hour before to set the place up and get organised. But what was more alarming was the fact Lee said Libby was there. Libby would be able to take one look at her face and know something was up. "Libby's here?" she squeaked, feeling the beginnings of the wine hitting her bloodstream.

"You bet your arse Libby is here," came the gleeful voice from behind Lee, who was still looking suspiciously at her.

Ivory forced back a shiver at Libby's gleeful tone. *One look and she already knows,* she thought. She knew Ivory had spent the night in deviant bliss with three different penises at the same time. She'd rather have them believe she was an alcoholic. Libby was going to be merciless. She attempted to make a lame excuse to flee. "I was just—"

"Investigating how much gooseberry is in our most expensive wine. I heard. I'll help you." She gave Lee a none-too-gentle shove before closing the door soundly in his face and leaning back against it.

Was it Ivory's imagination, or did Libby look a little demonic in this light? She backed away slowly, holding the bottle of wine as if it were a shield. "Now Lib . . ."

Her friend stalked her across the room. "Don't you use that placating tone on me, you little hussy. I know that look. You had sex!" Libby yelled.

Ivory shook her head. "I have no idea what you're talking about!"

"Don't bullshit a bullshitter. You totally banged someone!"

"Shh! Would you keep your voice down?!" she whisper-shouted at her bestie, glancing at the door.

"Sorry, sorry. It's just that my level of excitement is, like, high," Libby enthused, making Ivory smile despite herself. "Well, tell me. Which one was it?"

Ivory blushed furiously, mentally cursing the fair,

freckled face of her glamour. Why hadn't she chosen a darker complexion?

"Wait, don't tell me . . ." Libby studied her face for a moment, running critical eyes over her entire appearance. "Was it all of them? Oh my god! It was all of them, wasn't it? Holy shit! This is amazing!"

Ivory took a decent swig from the bottle clutched in a death grip in her hands. "Huh? What? What makes you say that?"

"Because you have the look that only the truly well-fucked can have," her filthy, plain-spoken friend assured her.

"Libby!"

"Well, it's true. Not that I would know. I haven't worn that look in years," she lamented. "How was it?"

Ivory groaned. "Libby . . ."

"Come on, my little sex demon. Help a sister out." She batted her eyelashes, looking pathetic, and Ivory completely lost it.

She began laughing hysterically over the ludicrousness of the situation. Libby joined in, grabbing the bottle from her and taking a healthy swallow. And this right here was exactly what she needed, she realised. She didn't need the quiet or solitude with her thoughts. She just needed her politically incorrect best friend, a bottle of wine, and a chance to talk about the sexual aptitude of the three men upstairs. And for the next twenty minutes, that's exactly what she did.

"Well, I don't know about you, but this has totally made my day," Libby informed her, polishing off the last of the bottle.

Ivory snorted. It had totally made her day, too, when she first awoke. Now she was halfway to drunk at ten in the morning with three men in her apartment who wanted to be tied to her forever because a damn cat said so. But if they were going to be tied to her with anything other than a coven bond, she wanted it to be because they liked her – the same way she liked them.

"Dammit, Ivory!" Libby's voice interrupted her introspection. "I know that look too. You're thinking too much again."

"I guess I am," she admitted, beginning to feel annoyed with herself.

"Tell me what's rattling around in that head of yours."

Ivory hesitated. "It's nothing."

"Now you listen here." Libby grabbed her shoulders and gave her a small shake that had her stomach revolting a little over the wine breakfast. "It's not nothing if it's bothering you. So spill. Besides, you just told me the length and girth of your three lovers' dicks. I think we're a little past withholding information."

She giggle-snorted over that. Libby did have a point. "I like them."

Libby pursed her lips. "Well, considering you screwed their brains out, I'd say that's a good thing."

"No, Libby. I like them as in I *like* them," she emphasised, so Lib would catch her drift.

"Oh . . . which one?"

"All of them."

"Oh."

"Exactly."

"Well, I say this is a good thing. I've never heard you say you like anyone before. Looks like all your Christmases have come at once." Libby patted her knee. "Don't overanalyse it. Just let it be for now," she advised.

It was actually good advice, but Ivory was a do-er, and an impatient one at that. When she had a problem, she wanted it resolved immediately. Besides, that wasn't the bulk of the problem. "It's not just that, Libby. They—" She desperately wanted to confess everything to her good friend but knew she had to hold back. "They found out something about me – something I've never told anyone," she ended with a half-truth.

Libby's clear-blue eyes focused on her intently for a moment. "I assume you're talking about what you're running from? I'm not stupid, Ivory. I notice things. I've known you were hiding something for a while now. And no, I don't want to know." She held up a hand, forestalling Ivory's nervous response. "People have secrets. It's okay. Lord knows I have my fair share."

Ivory studied her friend, and for the first time, she saw sadness in her eyes. Had she been so focused on keeping her own secrets, holding onto her own problems, that she'd failed to see her friend was also in pain? "I'm sorry, Lib. I—"

But Libby slapped her hand over her mouth. "Ivory, please. We're all good. I won't pester you and you won't pester me. Cool?"

"Cool," she agreed, still feeling a little ashamed and like she was betraying their friendship by not revealing her true self. But the revelation that Ronan, Vaughn, and Seth were familiars – *her* familiars – and somehow also mates to her inner panther . . . ? Well, it was about all she could handle today.

"Okay, without telling me what your fine bodyguards have discovered, tell me how they reacted. I assume not well if you're so anxious about it."

Ivory thought about their reactions – shock and awe pretty much covered it. "On the contrary, they said all the right things . . . again."

"Okaaay . . . So, what? You're back to not believing them again?"

"That's just the problem – I do believe them." Her shoulders slumped. "I'm worried I can't be what they need."

That much was true, at least. Even in her state of shock, she wasn't oblivious. She had seen the fragile hope on Vaughn's face, the sheer joy on Seth's, and the tentative look of expectation in Ronan's eyes. They had said she was a miracle. How was she supposed to live up to those kinds of expectations?

Her mother had told Ivory what little her father passed on to her. She understood that a familiar's urge to serve their coven and their witch was ingrained bone deep. It was a duty and an honour they were born with. The three men upstairs were born knowing their purpose in life but had been unable to fulfil it. For men of action, she knew the waiting and the fruitless searching must have been hell. Was she supposed to just magically fix that? She was naturally very magically inclined. Her mother had always been surprised at how powerful her magic had been as a child. Especially given they had no coven to study and practice with. But her abilities didn't matter if she didn't understand the rules or the politics of the game. She had never been immersed in the magical world. She was pretty much clueless.

"Ivory. Just let yourself be. Don't force anything. Things have a tendency to work out the way they're supposed to in the end."

Libby imparted her final piece of Yoda-like advice before pushing up and leaving her alone in the cellar with an empty wine bottle and a head spinning with more than just alcohol.

Twenty~One

"Y ou shouldn't have let her go," Seth groused, pacing the length of the room.

"Did it look like we had a choice?" Vaughn snapped back from where he was standing stiffly by the window.

"She's confused and scared. We shouldn't leave her alone," Seth pushed again.

Ronan shook his head. "She's overwhelmed. She needs time without us complicating things. She seems to do enough of that on her own anyway," he added, frowning over Ivory's continuous questioning and second-guessing. It was rather annoying. "Besides, she's just downstairs like she said she was going to be. Can't you feel her magic?"

Since they had a chance to see and feel her

powers, Ronan could sense her magic easily. The magical bond was there now and would be until the day they died. He was definitely a familiar to her witch.

Seth frowned but at least stopped his agitated movements. "Is that what that is? That low-level buzz in my body?"

"Yeah, that's what it is. It's normal for familiars and their witches. We'll know it if she decides to be an idiot and leave. We've been around the block a few times. We know what we're talking about." Vaughn sounded pompous and arrogant – a sure-fire way to piss Seth off further.

"Really, Vaughn? You're going to throw that in my face? So I've never served a witch before. You both have dozens of times, *blah, blah, blah*. It doesn't mean you know more about this particular situation than me," Seth barked.

Vaughn looked bored with the whole conversation – another deliberate act to fuel the flames. "Um, yeah. Pretty sure it does, kid."

Seth growled out his retort. "Don't call me kid!"

Vaughn shrugged. "Then don't act like one."

Seth's top lip lifted, exposing his sharpened canines as his growl intensified, rumbling low in his throat. Ronan stood up and walked between the pair, blocking them from each other's line of sight. "Stop posturing – the both of you. We have bigger things to worry about than you two acting like toddlers." But Ronan saw the calculation in Seth's eyes and knew his intervention was going to be for naught.

"I was right, by the way. When are you going to admit that? Huh, fellas? Not only is there a witch from our coven still alive, but that witch is Ivory. Come on, say it: Seth. Was. Right," Seth taunted, and Ronan just shook his head, not even bothering to stop Vaughn this time. Seth was pretty much asking for it – no matter how right he was.

Vaughn rushed past him in a blur, tackling Seth and taking him to the ground. "Watch the furniture," he cautioned the grappling pair, observing them mildly as they rolled back and forth on Ivory's magenta rug. Such a display had been a common occurrence when they had first decided to be together. They'd both mellowed a little over the years, but you couldn't put two, well three, alphas together and not expect a bit of conflict.

The pair continued to roll around for a minute before Vaughn dragged Seth up to his knees, planting a hard, punishing kiss to his lips. Seth arched into him for a split second before rumbling and pulling away, nimbly gaining his feet. Vaughn lunged at him again, but Seth was quicker this time. He side-stepped and Vaughn hit the wall with a loud thud. Ronan winced – he really hoped they didn't break anything.

"What is going on in here?!"

All three of them spun to see Ivory standing in the doorway, brown eyes wide in disbelief as she took in the scene.

"Just boys being boys," he assured her, looking warningly at his two lovers. Seth now had Vaughn pinned to the wall and was grinding his hips against the other man whilst attacking his neck. Vaughn was sure to have one hell of a hickey. Ivory looked a little wide-eyed, poised on the doorstep. The right word would have her stepping over the threshold, and the wrong one would send her bolting.

"Care to join us?" The breathless, taunting comment came from Vaughn.

Ronan merely let his head fall to his chest; those had been the wrong words. Sure enough, Ivory spun on her heels and fled as if the hounds of hell were chasing her.

"Damn you, Vaughn! You scared her off!" Seth accused, pushing him roughly away.

"It was more likely seeing you throw Vaughn against the wall and bite into his neck like some sort of savage that scared her off," Ronan pointed out long-sufferingly.

"No. It definitely wasn't that," Vaughn stated, leaning lazily against the battered wall. He looked sexy and smug, and definitely more relaxed now. He continued, "Don't you smell that? That woman is hotter than hell right now."

Ronan inhaled deeply, immediately groaning out loud as the luscious scent of feminine lust and desire filled his nostrils. He was forced to adjust his hardness as he watched Seth do the same.

"We should go after her." Seth's voice was raspy with lust.

"Maybe just one of us," Ronan suggested. "No point overwhelming the poor woman more."

"I'll go," Seth immediately piped up.

"I think I should go. You two have already put on enough of a show." His reprimand held no real heat. The two of them were never going to change, and he never wanted them to anyway. He loved everything about them – even their bullheadedness.

"You just want an opportunity to be alone with her."

Was that a pout on Seth's handsome face? Ronan raised an eyebrow at him. "Maybe I do. Is that a problem?"

"Not with me. Your cat is the most mellow out of the lot of us. You're the most likely to make it through a conversation without jumping her bones." Seth shrugged, morphing back to the easy-going man he was the majority of the time.

"Fine with me too. Besides, I have unfinished business with the kitten here."

Ronan watched as Vaughn allowed a real growl to rumble in his chest while he pursued Seth, unbuttoning his jeans and backing the man into a corner. Seth's eyes sparked with defiance once more, but this time it was playful as he made a pathetically fake attempt to dodge a stalking Vaughn.

Ronan smirked, locking the door behind him as he left his two lovers grappling for dominance in Ivory's lounge room. Going by the lengthening of Vaughn's canines as he stalked Seth across the room, Ronan was betting on him winning this round.

Once outside, he raised his face to the sky, scenting the air in an attempt to determine the direction Ivory had fled. He could use the magical connection just as easily – familiars had built-in radars where their witches were concerned. It helped them in their service and duties. But his panther demanded the more intimate mate-bond in order to track their wayward female. The lingering scent of rain, grass, and vanilla mixed with heat was a heady combination, and he took off in a steady jog, following the smell towards the woods that surrounded the edge of the bar's carpark.

Ivory must have been moving at a reasonable pace, for he soon found himself immersed in the dense trees and bushland of the wooded reserve. He frowned, picking up his pace a little, concerned about Ivory being alone in such a remote area. The woman was being stalked, after all. The reminder sent a chill down his spine and had his panther rising possessively to the surface. The beast wanted to hunt the female down, pin her beneath him, and mark her so others knew she was taken. It also wanted its female to acknowledge who was in charge. Ronan was going to have to have words with his inner animal because he had no doubt Ivory was going to be well and truly in charge of all of them. He shook himself, lecturing his animal briefly about control. The last thing he wanted to do was scare the flighty woman further. He highly doubted that seeing him turn into a seven foot long, ninety kilo-gram black jungle cat would fill her with confidence when she had expressed her disdain over the whole mate thing.

The track he was on was quite well worn,

suggesting it was used fairly regularly. In fact, the walking track and surrounding vegetation were practically saturated with Ivory's scent, and he realised this must be the route she took for her runs – both human and animal. He knew how crazy he got when he didn't allow his panther out to run and hunt. No doubt, Ivory's was the same, and it now made sense why she had chosen to put down roots in this area. The wooded forest appealed to his cat on a primal level. It was dark and dense, the smells strong and earthy. And he could hear numerous small prey animals scurrying around.

The human half of him that was her bodyguard found himself even more annoyed and bothered – routines were a stalker's wet dream. Plus, when they had asked her about her habits, she hadn't mentioned frequenting these woods at all. They couldn't protect her properly if she kept leaving things out. It didn't matter that she had no doubt failed to disclose her frequent forest jaunts because she could shapeshift into a big white cat. But now that everything was out in the open, they were going to talk all this shit through. No more running, no more hiding – for any of them.

Seeing movement up ahead, he breathed out in relief. Ivory was sitting on a fallen log, her leg bouncing in clear agitation. "Ivory! You promised us you wouldn't leave the bar. It isn't safe." He did his best to use his stern voice when all he wanted was to drag her to him and hold her tight.

"I know, I'm sorry. And I know I keep saying that too. I do mean it every time. I just . . ." She waved her hands around her head. "Libby says I think too much. She says I should just focus on being a little hussy and let sleeping cats lie." She snorted indelicately. "Sleeping cats!" she repeated, before giggling a little sloppily.

He leaned in closer, catching a whiff of a suspiciously familiar scent. "Wait . . ." He sniffed at her lips. "Are you drunk?"

She straightened her shoulders, trying – and failing – to look pious. "Not all the way."

"Bloody hell, woman! It's not even midday," he exclaimed.

"And? What's your point? Why do people always say that? Your taste buds don't care what time it is. They don't have a schedule, you know. It's like only eating cereal at breakfast time. Why is that? Who says it's a morning food? What if I want to eat cereal for dinner? I should be allowed to without justifying myself. Just like I should be allowed to gauge the gooseberry content of my wine when I want to."

Ivory prattled on somewhat incoherently, and he found himself quite enamoured by her tipsy ramblings coupled with the defence of her logic. She was rather adorable.

Deciding sometimes actions were far wiser than words, he grabbed her by the shoulders and hauled her up. Seizing her lips with his own, he nearly whimpered as her sweet flavour burst over his taste buds. He discovered there was indeed a hint of gooseberry adding a delicious spice to the kiss. She opened her mouth willingly, thrusting her tongue seductively against his own. Groaning, he fumbled with the hem of her shirt, pushing it up and out of the way so he could access the surprisingly lush breasts he had discovered the night before. Ivory moaned into his mouth, arching her body into his. He felt her nipple pebble against his palm, and he used his thumb to brush teasingly over the hard peak.

"Wait . . . no . . . stop." Ivory's hands were suddenly pushing him away instead of pulling him close.

He raised his head immediately but shook it. "Don't tell me to stop." He didn't know how much longer he could be patient with her continued hot and cold treatment.

"But this is wrong." Her breathless voice whispered over his flesh like a caress.

His hand was still cupping the weight of one generous breast, and he allowed his fingers to give the warm mound a gentle squeeze. "It's the rightest thing in the whole world," he assured her. "Does it feel wrong?"

She shook her head but didn't answer him. He tried not to let his frustration show in his voice as he pressed on. "After you had your chat with Vaughn, you said you were willing to give this a chance. Give *us* a chance. And these last few days – getting to know you, being in your space with your scent and your warmth – it's been heaven. You've enjoyed it too, I know you have." And he did. He'd lost count of the number of times he would catch her eyeing one of them when she thought no-one was looking.

She was a strong woman, full of fire and life. She was independent, smart, and decisive in everything she did. He couldn't understand where her reticence was coming from, especially after the earth-shattering experience of last night. "And what about last night, hmm? You shared your body with us, and ours with yours. It was something special."

"I know. I know that, Ronan. And I'm not trying to be a silly little girl about everything. It's just . . . I need to know you all feel the same way I do. Is it just obligation? For one thing, you are my bodyguards."

He was quick to respond. "We would never allow our personal feelings to interfere with our job. Keeping you safe is our top priority. This isn't just a proximity thing or a damsel in distress thing. If that was the case, there were countless times we would have slept with our clients – both males and females. It's not a protector complex."

She searched his eyes for a moment before finally nodding. "Okay – not a 'save the little woman' complex. But what about the mate thing? Is it just scratching a primal itch?"

She was insecure. So very insecure. How could he and the others not have seen that before? He placed his palms on either side of her face, forcing her eyes to his. "Ivory, a bunch of pheromones can't manufacture emotions. I have feelings for you, as do Seth and Vaughn. Hell, you're all we ever talk about when we're alone now: did you know Ivory does this? Did you see Ivory do that? Did you hear Ivory say this? Honestly, it's a little pathetic." He smiled with a hint of bashfulness. "Everything I've seen, everything I've heard about you – I like it all. I just plain like you, Ivory. And I know the others feel the same way. We all fell for you well before we knew you were a witch and a potential mate."

She reached up and covered his hands with her own, looking deeply into his eyes. "Okay."

"Okay?" he repeated. What did that mean?

She nodded. "Okay. I believe you. I believe *in* you." She took a deep breath and stepped back. "So let's figure out who the hell has been doing these things to me, so we can focus on what the hell we're going to do about us."

He remained silent as they walked back to her home hand in hand, cautioning himself about priorities. The situation with the stalker had become worryingly serious. Whoever it was had well and truly snapped, and he had no doubt that the guy's infatuation with Ivory wasn't going to be enough for him now. Capturing her and forcing her acknowledgement of their connection wasn't going to satisfy him as it once would have. Now, only Ivory's death would bring her stalker satisfaction. But he didn't say that out loud, nor did he tell her what he and his mates were going to do about her, even though he already knew.

They were going to keep her.

Twenty-Two

After picking up Ivory's business mail at the post office, Seth decided to take the scenic route through the woodlands that skirted the whole town and edged Ivory's property. He had already opened all the mail, finding only bills and catalogues. Nothing from their new mystery man.

There had been no more contact since the lewd photos and removal of the cameras, but Ivory had taken a few days off work anyway. She had been more shaken than she had let on – and so had he. The thought of some sick fuck invading her privacy that way and making her feel unsafe and uncomfortable in her own home made him wish he could hunt the fucker down and gut him with his dew claw.

Ivory had been a little more subdued at first, when she and Ronan walked back in the morning of the big revelations. She had been somewhat fidgety and uncomfortable – shy almost. It didn't help that she was a little drunk. But at least she hadn't pulled away from them.

The four of them spent the last three days talking so much that even he had a sore throat. They had discussed all things witch and familiar, answering Ivory's relentless questions and asking their own. Not that he could blame her. Her mother had done the best she could, given her own parents had died when she was so young. But her knowledge base was severely limited. Not that Ivory's magical abilities appeared to be diminished by her ignorance and lack of a mentor. The woman was wicked strong.

She seemed to be taking the whole familiar thing in stride, thankfully. Not that he was all that surprised. The connection between a witch and their familiar was organic, as natural as breathing. So she wasn't finding it too difficult to adjust to having them around and knowing them in that capacity. The mate thing, on the other hand? Well, that was a different story. She still had reservations about their panthers wanting to claim her as their life-mate. She admitted she could accept the insane attraction they all had to each other as a chemical reaction, but that it wasn't enough for her. She wanted them to get to know the real her more before anything further happened.

He was trying very hard not to get frustrated with her. He knew he didn't just want her because his cat's pheromones demanded it. The night spent in her arms had been one of the best of his life. And the fact that he had been able to share it with the men he loved had made it even more special. But he wasn't falling for what she could offer them between the sheets. He was falling for the stubborn, feisty, generous, funny, brave woman. He could only hope she was falling for them in the same way. And given she had promptly called for a moratorium on all things sex, they'd had nothing but time to connect on a more mental and emotional level, anyway.

The look of devastation on Vaughn's face when Ivory had primly told them they would not be sharing her magnificent round bed with her had been almost comical. But after three days of being in Ivory's presence, with her natural white hair, exotic purple eyes, and inhaling her scent, it thoroughly killed his amusement. He was walking around with a constant hard-on, and he was afraid his balls would be a permanent blue colour.

To make matters worse, he wasn't even getting any relief from his men. They had stupidly decided they would all wait for Ivory to feel comfortable before being together again. It had been Ronan's idea – the annoyingly mature bastard – and had seemed like the noble thing to do at the time. But now . . . now he wasn't feeling so noble.

A loud ding from his phone was a welcome distraction from the state of his neglected dick, and he fished it out of his pocket. That ding was the notification sound for his emails. He had gotten in contact with a fellow familiar and friend who worked for one of the founding covens. Spencer had access to all information of historical significance, and Seth had asked him to discreetly investigate Dale and Maree. Had there been any mention of them being more than casual lovers in the history books? Any suspicion that Dale had faked his own death? Had there been any indication that the conclave knew Maree was pregnant and had indeed threatened them? And most importantly, was there any mention of Ivory anywhere?

When Ronan had suggested they make some gentle enquiries, Ivory had freaked out on them again. Her aversion to the conclave was deeply ingrained, and they had almost caved and abided by her wishes to make no attempt to investigate. After all, as familiars, they were bound to do what their witch wanted in all things. But Seth had persevered, assuring her he would be discreet and only contact someone he trusted. His gut was telling him there was something going on – some kind of connection. And he always trusted his gut. It had led him to Ronan and Vaughn, and now Ivory. As far as he was concerned, that was a pretty good track record.

The feeling was cemented when Ivory had admitted she'd felt like she was being followed five years ago, and that's why she'd decided to move on and build a new life for herself here in Hadleigh. Seth could have shaken her when he heard that. Why hadn't she mentioned it before? Oh, he knew she believed then and now were two unrelated things – that her stalker was just some random, infatuated, crazy arsehole. And that was most likely the case, especially when she tried to appease him by saying the watcher from her past hadn't felt malicious. It had just been enough to make her feel uncomfortable, and that she had been discovered, and it was time to move on and make a new face. But Seth's gut wasn't convinced.

He tapped his little inbox icon and read the contents of the email from Spencer. His gut clenched unhappily now – sometimes he hated being right. There was evidence that a witch marshal had been sent out five years ago to Arland – the city Ivory had been living in – to investigate rumours of a rogue witch. The marshals were witches who acted like the police of their society. They made sure their laws were upheld, criminals were incarcerated, and that witch hunters were dealt with swiftly. They were also responsible for making sure no rogue witches were roaming unchecked in the world and putting their hidden society in danger.

The marshal who had been in charge of investigating whether there was a real witch in Arland had reported no evidence of one. His official report to the conclave had stated Ivory was a mere wiccan with no magical powers at all. The conclave had clearly taken him at his word because there had been no further investigations into a rogue witch in five years. But six months ago, the conclave had enlisted the exact same marshal to look into the small town of Hadleigh. A witch passing through the town had spotted an authentic cauldron in a pub coincidentally called the Hex Bar and had reported it. As Vaughn would say, coincidences were fucking suspicious.

But what confirmed it for Seth was Spencer's last

sentence of his email: *'No evidence of a witch – rogue or otherwise – in the township of Hadleigh.'*

The exact same marshal had falsified the report once again. There was definitely a witch in Hadleigh. He was speed dialling Ronan when a twig snapping behind him had him spinning around and reaching for the gun in the waistband of his pants. But before he could even close his hand over the butt of the gun, a crushing blow to his head landed him on all fours, literally seeing stars. A second whack, this time to his temple, had blackness clouding his vision in seconds.

Dammit! I really hate being right all the time.

Twenty-Three

I vory paced in her living room. She felt edgy
and unsettled and didn't know why. She and
the boys had been shut inside her apartment
for the past three days as they put every resource
towards finding her stalker.

They had reached out to all their contacts –
witch, familiar, and human alike – to gather information. So far, they had come up with exactly zip.
The cameras were indeed military grade, but their
origin and purchase couldn't be placed. They had no
luck tracing the stationary used – it was generic and
could be bought from any supermarket in the country. There were no prints, and the DNA left on the
underwear she had received wasn't in any database.

What's more, their panthers hadn't been able to detect or follow any scent.

With three days of seclusion, she hadn't needed to use her glamour, and her magic was recuperating. She'd been doing her own research into spells, and she finally convinced them to allow her to scry for the location of the stalker. It wouldn't reveal his identity, but she should be able to find his where-abouts. They were going to give it a try just as soon as Seth returned from the post office.

"Hey, what's wrong?" Ronan asked, engulfing her from behind in his strong arms.

She shook her head. "I don't know. My cat is restless. Something's wrong. I can feel it."

"I'm sure it's nothing. My cat gets that way some-times when it's cooped up for too long. We haven't been outside much recently. She probably just needs a good run," Ronan assured her.

It made sense. Her panther did get restless when she didn't shift for long periods of time. It was one of the reasons why she had chosen this location for her home. The dense forest at the base of the moun-tain appealed to her cat on every level. But this didn't feel like she wanted to go on a hunt. This was more of a nervous tension. Like she was waiting for something to happen. An air of repressed violence had hung like a sinister cloud ever since receiving the photos. And she had a feeling it wasn't going to stay repressed for much longer.

A sudden loud bang had her jumping like a startled rabbit.

"Easy. It's just Vaughn. He doesn't know how to close doors quietly, like a normal human being," Ronan joked.

Sure enough, Vaughn stomped his way into the room. "Hey, what's up?" he asked, picking up on her obvious tension.

Ronan rubbed her shoulders in comfort and answered, "Ivory's panther is feeling a bit jumpy. Needs to get out."

"It's not that," she declared, shrugging away from him. "Something's wrong. Where's Seth?" she asked suddenly.

"He's fine. He was going to pick up your work mail and grab a few supplies, remember? He'll be back soon," Vaughn assured her.

"That only takes a few minutes – it's not far. How long since you last saw him?" That nervous feeling was now turning into anxiety.

Before any of them could answer, Ivory's phone beeped with an incoming text. She eyed the phone as if it were a snake about to strike – it was bad news.

She could feel it. With trembling hands, she picked it up – and promptly felt her stomach drop when she saw Seth's number. Opening the message, she read: *'I have one of your rent boys. The woods. Ten minutes. Come alone or more of this . . .'*

Less than a second later, her phone vibrated and pinged once again – only this time a photo immediately popped up on the screen.

Her breath rushed from her lungs, her muscles going lax as the phone dropped from her hands and clattered to the floor.

"Ivory! Ivory, what is it?" Ronan's voice sounded tinny in her ears as she sucked in air, trying to get ahold of herself. Now was not the time to fall apart. She needed her anger – not her fear.

A spine-chilling roar echoed around the room, forcing Ivory's eyes up and past a concerned-looking Ronan who was kneeling in front of her. Vaughn had picked up her phone and seen what she had; Seth, bruised and bloody, was pinned to a tree, his left hand impaled with a knife into the trunk behind him. His eyes were closed – he must have passed out. At least Ivory hoped he was only passed out. The alternative didn't bear thinking about. Besides, her stalker – whoever it was – was obviously using Seth as leverage. He wouldn't kill him. He needed him.

Brushing aside Ronan's hand, she stood, firming her jaw. "I have to go."

Vaughn met her eyes as Ronan snatched the phone from his hands, a low whine sounding from his chest. Vaughn's eyes were glowing with his inner animal – a pure predator ready to hunt and destroy the adversary who had dared touch his mate. Ivory knew hers were the same, and as she looked towards Ronan, his claws were out and flexing as if he were already envisioning her stalker's death.

"Let's go," he growled.

Ivory's heart stuttered. She was not jeopardising anyone else she loved – wait, *loved?* Did she love them? She wondered one second and then realised that yes, she did – so very much – in the next second. She loved them. All three of them. They were hers and she was theirs, and there was no way she was allowing any of them to get hurt more because of her. She raised her chin. "He said to come alone. I'm going alone."

The tension in the room seemed to cause the walls to expand and the air to thin. Both Ronan and Vaughn had stilled at her words. Ivory had one second to gulp before they both stalked forwards, reaching her in two strides. They backed her into the wall behind her – dominant alphas enforcing their will over their woman. Ivory shivered, her body responding to the display, with her nipples tightening and her sex clenching hungrily. It was completely inappropriate, and they didn't have time for this, but she simply couldn't help it. Her breath quickened and she licked her lips, two sets of green eyes following the movement as if entranced.

"You're not going anywhere." Vaughn's voice was so gravelly she could barely make out the words.

Eyeing his mouth, she figured it was probably due to the fact that his canines had extended and were pressing against his bottom lip. A quick glance to her left revealed Ronan was in a similar state, his chest expanding under the force of his breathing, and his height towering over her as his animal exerted its dominance.

She had to stop this before things got too out of control – they were acting on their instincts right now. Their animals were in charge, in fear for their mate, and although she understood it – *felt* it – she needed the men to be in charge. Besides, she wasn't willing to be a submissive mate, obeying her male partners' every command just because she was the only female in the shadow. She had been taking care of herself since she was eighteen. She was a strong, independent woman and a powerful witch on top of all that. She really wished her powers would work on them so she could flatten them to a wall until they calmed down. But after a few days experimenting with them, she had accepted the fact that they had been telling the truth – her telekinesis and her spells had no effect on any of them. That only left her words as a weapon.

"I need you to listen to me . . ." she began.

Twin growls met her ears, causing goose bumps to erupt over her skin. "No, Ivory. We're done listening and you're done talking. We've done things your way and done nothing but talk and listen for days. It's our turn now," Vaughn informed her.

She tried to open her mouth again, only to find it crushed by his mouth. His plundering was swift but thorough and she was left breathless when he pulled back, tugging on her hair to keep her attention. "We are going to shift and follow you into the forest. End of discussion."

His arrogant tone made her hackles rise. "He said to come alone. Are you willing to risk Seth's life for mine?"

"Yes. You are our woman, our female. Seth would expect nothing less." Ronan pinned her to the spot with his words. "No-one will see us, and no-one will be expecting two panthers to be there anyway," Ronan pointed out.

Ivory's reactive fear decreased a little when she heard that logic. He was right. Although she could hardly believe they would be willing to risk losing their long-term lover just to keep her safe, she couldn't help the way her heart skipped a giddy beat upon hearing the words. They loved her too. They must. Without further ado, the two men she loved beyond comprehension shredded their clothes as they morphed into huge, sleek black panthers in her living room.

Her pulse picked up when she thought about that 'L' word again. She had only met them two weeks ago. She knew it was fast, but she wasn't going to diminish the moment by qualifying it in any way. Regardless of the exceptional, highly emotional circumstances they had met under, she realised none of that mattered. She loved them and she was going to revel in the discovery.

Just as soon as they got the fourth member of their quartet back.

Twenty~Four

I vory made her way quickly down the familiar path, keeping a sharp ear out for any noise to alert her to where Seth was being held. Her stomach was in knots, but she was also resolved; this would end today.

She knew Ronan and Vaughn were somewhere close in the dense trees because she could feel them. But she couldn't see them or hear them. They were truly predators stalking their prey. A small fork to the left caught her attention because of Seth's strong scent, and she hastened down it, her need to get to him rising more with each passing second. A few minutes later, she reached a small clearing and gasped, clutching her hands ineffectually.

Seth was still pinned to the massive tree with a

knife all the way to the hilt through his hand and into the thick trunk. He had a makeshift gag over his mouth and blood ran from a terrible head wound. He must have heard or sensed her because he opened his eyes, immediately shaking his head in agitation. She tried to tell him with her eyes that everything was going to be okay, that they had a plan. He had to know Vaughn and Ronan would never have allowed her to come on her own – despite the danger to themselves. They were hiding in the trees, watching and waiting for their chance to pounce.

Just then, Seth's beautiful green eyes, now blurry with pain, widened, and he tried to talk around the gag. She felt movement behind her and knew her stalker must be there. Plucking up her courage, she squared her shoulders and spun around slowly. She thought she was prepared to confront the person who had been terrorising her for the past few months. She was a strong, independent woman – *blah, blah, blah*. But the person standing in front of her was the last person she expected to see, and she blinked several times in confusion.

"Libby?" Her employee, her confidant, her best friend, simply stood in the middle of the clearing, not saying anything. Her face was a blank, emotionless mask, and her lively blue eyes looked dead. "No." Ivory shook her head. *This isn't possible. It can't be Libby!* her heart screamed, but her brain registered otherwise. "How could you do this?" she cried.

"She didn't. Well, not alone anyway."

The voice came from behind her and startled her so much, she fell backwards onto her butt. She recognised that voice. What the hell was going on here? How could she have misjudged these people so gravely? "Lee?"

"Got it in one, babe." He walked to her slowly, bending down to touch her cheek. She flinched under the light caress, her stomach revolting, and he gave her a sharp slap. "Bad Ivory," he reprimanded, just as he had in the notes and phone calls.

She was in such a state of shock that she barely felt the sting from his hand. Her men must have taken exception to the treatment, however, because they exploded from the trees, leaping with claws outstretched, ready to take off Lee's head . . . only to be brought up short by an invisible force that lifted them up and flung them away as if they weighed nothing. They landed with sickening force on the hard ground, yelping. But that didn't stop them, only seemed to enrage them further, and they were back on their feet in seconds.

Lee sighed, weaving an intricate but invisible sign in the air, and the two panthers began to writhe in agony. "Stop! Stop it!" she screamed, launching herself at her tormentor. But before she could make contact, a leg swept out and knocked her back down.

"Stay down." Libby's voice was cold and flat.

Ronan's and Vaughn's furious growls abruptly cut off, and she turned her head quickly to find them both panting on the ground. At least they were still breathing. She turned back to Lee, and his face was twisted into an evil sneer, his blue eyes dancing with sadistic pleasure.

"You're a witch?" She knew her voice sounded incredulous – it was exactly how she felt.

"Give the lady a gold star." He clapped slowly. "Oh, come now. Don't look so surprised. After all, you're a witch too," he pointed out.

She cursed internally. She was a witch. She had magic. Why was she just sitting here acting helpless while her lovers were being hurt? Lee must have seen the intent in her eyes, for he slapped her again – harder this time. It was enough to cause her to lose her concentration, and before she could recover, he had Seth by the hair with a knife to his throat.

"Let's not try anything silly, sweetheart. I'd love

to feel lover boy's hot blood pumping out over my boots."

She swallowed hard, looking into Seth's eyes and seeing no fear there. He would support her, whatever she chose to do. But in the end, she did the only thing she could. She held up her hands in surrender. "I won't try anything. I promise."

Lee tilted his head, considering her for a moment. "I'm going to take you at your word, Ivory. Don't disappoint me, okay?" He slashed the knife in a downward motion, causing Seth to flinch. The cut was shallow, but the warning was clear. Lee looked over to Vaughn and Ronan. "Shift now."

They seemed to struggle to heed his command, and Ivory realised they were still being held down by the spell Lee had performed. The moment they were human again, they were flung backwards onto their own trees, and once again imprisoned by invisible bonds.

"Good familiars. Stay." He laughed crazily at his own joke, finally releasing Seth's hair from his punishing grip. He walked over to her. "You know, I can't believe you managed to stumble across your familiars. Fate certainly has a wicked sense of humour. I believe you've already met mine . . ." He gestured to Libby.

Libby was Lee's familiar? Ivory had been hoping Libby was somehow a victim, just as much as she was. That Lee was holding something over her to make her do these terrible things. But she was wrong. Libby was Lee's familiar and must have been in on it the entire time. No wonder they could never piece together a proper timeline. Libby and Lee had always been able to provide alibis for each other. What's more, Libby had access to her apartment. Ivory had given her best friend a key. She felt the blade of betrayal slice right down to her core.

"As for further introductions, my name isn't really Lee – it's Matthew. I'm a marshal, sent here to determine if you are a rogue witch," he explained.

"Years ago, the conclave got word of a witch flying solo – no coven, no familiar. Can't have a witch running around on her own, performing magic and putting the witching community at risk, now can we? That didn't turn out so well in Salem." He laughed at that, as if the slaughter of their fellow witches was amusing to him. "You weren't as careful in Arland as you thought," he tsked, naming the city Ivory had lived in before here.

"I was tasked with finding the mysterious lone witch and determining if she was misusing her powers or harming people. It didn't take long to find you five years ago. You were using a pathetically weak glamour to mask your powers. By rights, I should have placed you into custody and taken you back to the conclave immediately after finding you."

"Then why didn't you?" she spat. If he wanted to reveal his whole evil plan, then she was happy to enable him. Anything to buy her some more time to come up with a way to escape and save her familiars. Besides, she was genuinely curious about the conclave sending a marshal after her. It sounded like they had no idea who or what she was. That they sent Lee – no, *Matthew* – after her only because she was a witch on her own. Could the boys be right when they said she didn't need to be afraid of the conclave?

Matthew strolled over to her, offering her a hand up. She wanted to tell him to shove his hand up his arse, but she forced herself to take it. He pulled her up and answered her previous question. "Because I could see straight through that glamour of yours. That hair, those eyes . . . you're a beautiful woman, Ivory. I wanted you," he stated simply, as if it made all the sense in the world. "Before I could even approach you, you fled. And this time, the glamour you used was a powerful one – I'll give you that. It was a bit trickier finding you, but eventually the conclave got a whiff of another lone witch. I volunteered, hoping it was you."

He picked up her hair, rubbing it over his cheek. "Five years is a long time to wait, Ivory," he pointed out. "You sure looked different than you had in Arland, but I'm a marshal. We're impervious to those types of spells – so those pesky criminals can't pull one over on us." He winked, and Ivory fought the urge to slap his handsome face. He was acting as if this was all some kind of game. As if he hadn't spent months befriending her, only to betray her with lies and fear.

"I'm not a criminal," she stated.

"No, my cohort here determined that before I even set foot in Arland all those years ago." He indicated to Libby, who was standing so quietly behind him that Ivory had almost forgotten she was there. "I sent Libby ahead of me to check things out. It only took her two days to figure out you weren't some magical menace."

It must have been Libby's presence she had felt five years ago, Ivory realised. No wonder she hadn't felt threatened. At the time, Libby wouldn't have had any malicious intent. But clearly, times had changed. Ivory's anger rose, and she clenched her fists, fighting the urge to use her powers.

"Uh, uh, uh, Ivory. Don't even think about it." Matthew wagged a finger at her. "I know you're an object mover – don't be getting any ideas now. I can crush their lungs with the snap of my fingers," he assured her, crooking a finger in Ronan's direction and causing him to cry out in pain as his body spasmed against the tree. Vaughn and Seth snarled at seeing their lover writhing in agony – helpless against their own bonds – and gained the attention of Matthew once again.

"You kitties want some more too?" he asked, grinning evilly and raising a hand in Vaughn's direction.

"Stop!" Ivory cried out. "Please, Le – Matthew. Stop." She wasn't above begging if it kept her family safe. Because her hands were her source of power, she held them out to the sides of her body. "I won't try anything, I promise."

"Damn right you won't." Matthew grunted, letting his hand fall to his side. She watched as Ronan's head fell forwards, his breathing rapid and blood streaming from his nose.

"Now, where were we?" he asked, reaching out to stroke her face, as if he couldn't resist touching her. "I saw you, Ivory, through that pathetically plain mask you put on for the world. And I just knew you had to be mine. I tried to be nice about it; I asked you out on a date, remember? But you said no, as if you were too good for the likes of me. ME!" he yelled abruptly, startling her back a step and eliciting growls from her men.

"Me – a powerful witch, a trusted marshal, respected by the conclave. Do you know what my record for retrieving rogue witches is? No need to guess, I'll tell you. One hundred percent. I am a warrior, Ivory. More than fit for a clueless witch like yourself. But you turned me down. Still, I gave you the benefit of the doubt." He began to pace in front of her as if he were a teacher giving a lecture, rather than a psycho holding them all captive with magic and pain. "I sent you flowers and chocolate and gifts – what woman doesn't like chocolate?" he asked conversationally.

"You sent me dead animals!" she snapped, feeling sick at the waste of life because of a madman.

"Well, I had to move on to Plan B when Plan A didn't work, didn't I? I tried to woo you – no deal. So I figured I'd scare you into my arms. *'Oh Lee, I'm so scared! There's a crazy person sending me drowned bunnies! I need your help, Lee. I need you!'*" he recited in a high-pitched voice. "But you didn't do that, did you, Ivory? No – you went and hired these three

Neanderthals instead. Useless, redundant creatures," he griped, literally spitting on Seth as he passed him. "Their bloodline is practically extinct. They failed in their duty. Pathetic."

This time, he kicked Seth solidly in the ribs as he passed, and Ivory's anger returned full force. "Don't!" she snapped.

Matthew spun fast, grabbing her face in one hand. "Don't?" he sneered. *"Don't?* Of course you wouldn't want me to hurt lover boy. I admit, when they first showed up, it pissed me off. And then when I realised you were spreading your legs for them . . . I've never felt so much rage before. You wouldn't even go out on a date with me, and yet you're quite happy to fuck animals. That's when I realised I had been going about this whole thing wrong."

He tightened his fingers on her face painfully. "You're a filthy slut, you see. A walking cunt who enjoys being gangbanged. You like it rough, bitch? Is that it? I was just too nice." He slammed his lips down on hers, teeth biting cruelly, his tongue forcing her mouth open.

She fought his hold, her hands gathering magic instinctively as she raised her leg to knee him in the junk. Hard hands grabbed her wrists as her captor chuckled, his hot breath fanning across her cheek and making her want to vomit. "Now, what did I say about using your magic?"

Fine, no magic, she thought, continuing to bring her knee up. He must have seen the intent in her eyes, though, because he twisted the lower half of his body and her knee landed harmlessly against his thigh.

"Naughty Ivory. You do like it rough, huh?" He let go of one of her hands, rubbing at his crotch grotesquely.

She turned her head away, worried she was going to vomit all over him. He was nuts – completely and utterly freaking insane. And very likely a sexual sadist as well. How had he hidden this side of himself so completely from her? She looked to her right, and Vaughn and Ronan were straining, still pinned to the thick tree trunks. They were snapping and snarling even in their human forms – their rage over hearing and seeing their mate reduced to a sexual object palpable. She knew if they were given even the barest chance, they would rip Matthew to literal shreds in seconds.

A small sound had her focusing on Seth. Although his green eyes were glacial, he wasn't raging like her other lovers. Instead, he looked calculating, shifting his focus northward in the direction of the knife impaled in his hand. Her gaze followed his and narrowed, understanding his meaning. *Clever kitty. Time to get them out of this mess,* she thought, renewed determination filling her. Her eyes sought Seth's, asking for permission and forgiveness at the same time. He gave a small nod of his head and she acted quickly, not willing to waste another second.

She stretched her free hand out, commanding the blade to rip out of wood and flesh, and sent it hurtling towards Matthew's exposed back.

"Look out!" Libby's voice shouted in warning.

Matthew spun, the knife embedding in his right shoulder instead of his heart, where she had been aiming. She glared in Libby's direction – betrayed again. A blinding blow sent her sprawling to the ground in a tangle of limbs and starbursts behind her eyelids. The prick had sucker punched her.

"Bitch!" he screamed, clutching his wounded shoulder. "I tried to be nice. I tried to be nice. I tried to be nice," he repeated over and over again, and Ivory realised he had completely snapped his leash.

Vaughn, Ronan, and Seth were all shouting, struggling futilely against Matthew's magical hold. Apparently, a knife in the shoulder wasn't enough to break the witch's concentration. She tried to raise her hands again, only to find them heavy and a sense a lethargy coming over her. What was happening?

"What's the matter, Ivory?" Matthew asked, bending over her. "Feeling sleepy?" He stroked a contradictory gentle hand over the slope of one breast. She couldn't even flinch away from the hated touch – she was that exhausted.

"Did I forget to mention what my main power was? I'm a syphon, Ivory. I can literally draw your magic from you."

Ivory's tears blurred her vision. *Powerless. She was powerless.*

Matthew laughed. "I guess you'll just have to lie there and take it, huh?" He stood and reached for the button on his jeans.

Her heart stuttered when she realised his intent, and her eyes automatically sought out her lovers. Their eyes were filled with impotent rage and anguish, as they continued to snarl, roar, and thrash. Blood was beginning to leak from their noses and eyes and she could see terrible bruises and lacerations splitting the skin of their necks and wrists as their bodies fought the magical bonds keeping them in place.

"Don't worry, boys. I'll let you watch while I fuck your tramp before I skin you all alive."

"Libby, please! Help us!" she yelled at her friend, frantic now for any kind of hope. She saw Libby flinch at her words, but she made no move to help, not even raising her head to look at her.

Matthew laughed again, the sound grating on Ivory's frayed nerves. "She won't help you. Libby's a good little familiar. She knows her place."

Ivory felt the last of her strength waning as blackness began to cloud her vision. What was she going to do? She had no magic, she was – *a complete fucking idiot!* She screamed suddenly, berating herself internally. Matthew said he was a syphon, draining her magic. Her telekinesis was a part of her magic. But . . . her panther was a part of *her*. She was her spirit animal, the second half of her soul. Her panther was her birthright from her grandmother's side. It didn't come from her grandfather's witch bloodline. And what was better? Matthew had no idea she was part familiar.

She focused her mind, and sure enough, there she was – a female predator ready to fight for herself and her mates. Ivory didn't hesitate, allowing her animal half to surface, rejoicing in the simplicity of the panther's mind: defend. It took mere seconds for the shift to be complete – her vision sharpened, sounds became acute – and she didn't hesitate, launching herself at her enemy.

The look of sheer shock on Matthew's face was laughable, but it was his scream of absolute terror that had her panther snarling in triumph. Her body twisted, ever agile, forcing him to the ground on his back. Her claws were burrowed in his chest and her teeth buried in his neck before he could call up his magic. The sharp, metallic taste of blood flooded her mouth and assaulted her senses, heightening the thrill of the kill. Her prey's frantic yelling and thrashing body almost dislodged her, but she hung on with her front paws, back paws bucking and digging at his sensitive, soft stomach.

Within seconds, the screaming was reduced to gurgles, then to a whistling sound . . . and then to nothing. When the body beneath her finally stopped moving, the white panther raised her face to the sky and roared her victory.

Twenty~Five

T he moment Ivory's teeth embedded in Lee's – or Matthew's – jugular, his hold over them broke. Ronan landed heavily on his knees but was up and running in a second, desperate to reach Ivory. He saw Vaughn do the same and gestured him in the direction of Seth, who was struggling to stand.

He heard the roar of victory, deafening in its intensity, and knew her prey must be dead. Seemed they were obsolete – completely useless, just as they had been when Matthew was hurting her. He wasn't sure he would ever get the images of that psycho touching her out of his head. But for now, he would try to be content with the knowledge that they were all safe.

He flung himself at the amazing white beast, her face and paws stained red with the blood of her tormentor. He was a little disappointed he wasn't the one to rip the piece of shit to shreds, but at least Ivory had gotten her vengeance. "Shift, babe. I need to see you," he said to the white jaguar purring under his stroking hands.

Seconds later, he had a handful of naked Ivory, and he couldn't help touching her and kissing her everywhere. More hands reached for her, and he snarled before reigning in his cat, recognising it was just Vaughn and Seth, their movements as equally desperate as his own.

"I'm okay, I'm okay," Ivory was repeating, stroking them and kissing them frantically in return. "Are you okay? Seth? Your hand!" She looked devastated as she gripped the bleeding appendage lightly.

Seth smiled, his eyes unfocused, and Ronan realised he likely had a concussion in addition to the damage done to his hand. "I'm fine," he assured them all.

Vaughn wrapped his arms around Seth, not letting go of Ivory's hand. His eyes were beseeching as they looked him over. Ronan understood exactly how he felt. He was never letting any of them out of his sight again.

"I'm sorry."

They all spun around, pushing Ivory into the middle of the circle of their bodies. Libby, the traitor, was on the ground crying. Ronan's lip lifted as he snarled. He wanted to subject her to the same fate as her master.

"Please, Ivory . . ." Libby sobbed. "let me explain."

"Shut up!" he yelled, seeing Ivory wince at the woman's words.

"Explain what? That you were never my friend? That you came here to set me up? That you let him terrorise me for months?" Ivory demanded, pushing them out of the way.

"Please, Ivory, you have to understand. I'm his familiar," Libby implored. "I did everything I could. I'm the one who told you to get help, remember? I gave you their number. I knew who they were. I knew they could help you. I did everything I could," she repeated, tears streaming down her face.

The new information seemed to give Ivory pause. "You knew who they were? You knew they were my familiars?"

"Well, no. Not that part. That must be fate or something. I just knew that they were the remaining familiars from the Panthera Coven. I knew they'd figure out a witch was behind all this, and I knew they'd be able to protect you."

Ronan grimaced. They hadn't figured out a witch was behind this, and they hadn't protected her.

"That doesn't make this okay. You betrayed me. You let him terrify me! You should have told me!" Ivory yelled.

"I couldn't! I'm his familiar!" Libby yelled back, as if that explained everything. And it kind of did – to Ronan anyway. But Ivory couldn't possibly understand, having never had a familiar before.

She confirmed his thoughts when she sneered, "What does that have to do with anything? You have free will, don't you? It's not like he was controlling you."

Libby pursed her lips and looked away, not saying anything.

"Ivory . . ." Ronan started, not wanting to defend the treacherous woman, but wanting to make sure his lady had all the facts. "She's his familiar."

Ivory released a sound of frustration, pulling at her glorious white hair. "Why does everyone keep saying that like it's the be all and end all?"

"Because it kind of is," he replied, taking her hand from her long locks and smoothing out her tightly clenched fingers. "Familiars and their witches are bound on a metaphysical level. We are everything our witch needs us to be: lover, friend, spy, murderer. We do have free will, but the innate desire to do the bidding of our witch and make them happy often overrides that. Especially if a witch is abusing their powers," he added, beginning to get a clearer sense of the situation now that the bloodlust was leaving his system.

Ivory frowned fiercely but seemed to be thinking. She looked to him, then Seth and Vaughn, who were still solid walls at her back. "Do you feel the need to obey me, no questions asked? Is that how it is with all familiars? Witches can just control them and make them do anything they want?"

Vaughn shrugged and answered her. "Pretty much. We live to serve our coven, our bloodline. Usually a witch doesn't ask anything of their familiar that they are not willing to do. But, if they do . . . our witch *can* force us."

"That's despicable!" Ivory's pale cheeks pinked in anger.

"It's just the way it is. Besides, usually a witch and their familiar are best friends. A witch wouldn't make their familiar do anything they didn't want to do. But . . . there are always exceptions," Seth said, looking towards Libby with a hint of pity.

"Is this true, Libby? Did Matthew force you?" Ronan hated seeing the tentative hope on Ivory's face. The betrayal from someone she considered a friend – family – was cutting her deep. He could tell she desperately wanted Libby to say yes. Hell – he was hoping and praying that Libby had been forced too. Otherwise, there would be no stopping Vaughn's panther from seeking retribution for hurting their mate. As it was, he wasn't sure it would be enough. Vaughn's panther was an aggressive bastard.

Libby's eyes darted fearfully to Matthew, who was virtually unrecognisable. "I'm his familiar," was all the woman said.

"Libby, look at me." Ivory stepped in front of her, sending Seth and Vaughn a quelling glance when they tried to hold her back.

"It doesn't matter," Libby muttered.

"Yes it does. It matters to me. And it's going to matter to the three big cats behind me too. Did he force you?"

"Yes! Of course, yes! I'm not some fucking psycho! I don't go around stalking people for fun! Matthew was a fucking bastard, okay?! He was an abusive, crazy prick! I hate him! Is that what you want to hear? I hate him!" Libby screamed, tears returning to stream down her face.

Ronan swallowed, making eye contact with the other two. Seth's eyes predictably held sympathy, and Vaughn's were still hard as flint, but they were now directed at the fallen witch. She was telling the truth – they could all scent it. And the one thing they all hated was abusive arseholes; they were protectors to their core. For a witch to abuse their familiar in such a way? It was despicable.

Ivory sighed, running her hands over Libby's hair. "Okay, Lib. It's going to be okay." She gestured with her head. "What do we do with him?" Ivory didn't even flinch as she looked towards the bloody remains of her tormentor.

Even Ronan winced when he saw the amount of blood pooling around Matthew's body – it was starting to congeal in the heat. What's more, the skin on his stomach had been completely shredded, causing his innards to now be *outtards*. But Ivory was looking at the messy remains with nothing more than curious disinterest. Female predators were darn scary, he thought, making a mental note to never piss off her inner cat. In fact, he would just start working on becoming her favourite right now.

He swept her up into his arms, causing her to yelp, and started making his way out of the woods. "Now we call the conclave and get them to deal with it," he told her. "And you – you are never leaving our sight again."

"Fuckin' A. You're to be within touching distance of one of us at all times," Vaughn commanded, supporting Seth with an arm around his waist.

"Preferably naked," Seth added, somehow managing to grin even with a knife-sized hole all the way through his hand.

In his arms, Ivory glowered. "You do realise I'm the one who saved all your arses, right? Why do I have to be the naked one?"

Ronan smiled down at her, stealing a kiss from her pouty lips. "Because you're the prettiest."

Twenty-Six

S ix hours later, Ivory was utterly exhausted. Once they had trekked back to her home above the bar, Ronan placed her in the shower before calling the witch conclave to report what had transpired.

She wasn't ashamed to admit she had curled up on the tile floor and allowed herself to bawl her eyes out for several minutes before agreeing with her cat and acknowledging she had no other choice. Lee – Matthew, whatever – would have raped her and killed her men, she had no doubt about that. Still – she had killed a man, and she was going to have to live with that.

She smiled, hearing the rumble of male voices down the hall. At least she wouldn't be living with it alone. She got the feeling she was going to have three very large, very possessive housemates who would support her through it . . . hopefully. It was one of the reasons why she was procrastinating in the kitchen, fiddling with the dirty dishes, instead of being in the bedroom with Vaughn, Ronan, and Seth.

It had taken less than an hour for two representatives from the conclave to show up. They were both marshals, and Ivory was happy to see they were not batshit crazy. Her three familiars had explained the situation in its entirety, from them taking on the job as her bodyguards, to discovering Ivory was a descendant of the Panthera bloodline, and finally Matthew's insanity and Libby's involvement.

An additional two marshals had arrived within another hour, with two senior witches and their familiars arriving a couple of hours after that. The mess that was her former stalker was dealt with in quick order – nothing like a little magic to clean up a crime scene. And the entire magical entourage had settled into her once spacious living room. With four marshals, three witches, and six familiars in it – including Libby – it hadn't seemed so roomy.

Ivory was saddened when she thought of her friend. The sassy, vibrant, mouthy woman she knew had disappeared beneath a guilt-ridden, tortured, broken person. The betrayal she felt over Libby's involvement cut deep, but what hurt worse was the knowledge of the abuse Libby had suffered at the hands of her witch. He should have been her greatest friend and ally – her *family.* But instead, he had abused his position and harmed that which was most precious: his familiar.

Ivory was feeling just as guilty over her ignorance. How could she not have known Libby was in trouble? Some friend she was. It just proved you never really knew what was going on behind closed doors. Libby had been taken by the marshals for further questioning, but Ivory fully intended to stay in touch. As far as she was concerned, they'd both kind of been shitty friends, what with the whole stalking thing on Libby's part and the obliviousness on Ivory's. They'd make it up to each other though.

The two witch representatives from the conclave had been extremely nice and sincerely shocked to learn of Ivory's story, especially the part where she had been hiding from them. They assured her that carrying familiar blood was rare, but by no means a punishable offence, and guaranteed her they would look into who had suggested such a thing in the first place. Ivory was dubious about believing them at first. Her mother, and her grandfather before her, had drilled the need to run and hide into her head from birth. Someone had cared enough about the purity of her bloodline that her grandfather felt the need to fake his own death. When she thought of all the years her mother had been scared of her own shadow, moving them from place to place, always looking over her shoulder for no reason? It made her sad beyond measure. It was such a waste of life.

Well, Ivory wasn't going to waste one more second. She had three hunks in her bedroom whom she loved deliriously. First, she was going to tell them. Second, she was going to bang their brains out. And third? She figured living happily ever after sounded just about right. Chuffed with her plan, she made her way down the hallway, pushing open the bedroom door . . . and coming to an abrupt halt.

Seth and Vaughn were gloriously naked, and Seth had Vaughn pinned below him on the mattress as he pounded into him with complete abandon. Ivory immediately grew wet as her senses went into hyperdrive; the musky scent of sex was ripe in the air, and the varying sounds of flesh slapping against flesh created an erotic symphony, tantalising and satisfying at the same time. Her gaze searched the corners of the room looking for her third man, and sure enough, there he was, naked and hard – eyes glowing with a sensual light as he palmed his own rigid length.

She knew they all had their kinks – *Woo hoo!* she celebrated silently – and Ronan's was watching. Yep – the chilled, quiet, peacekeeper of the group was a bit of a voyeur. It was always the quiet ones. But when in a relationship with three other people, Ivory figured it really worked out well. She'd never really given much thought to voyeurism before – had hardly even watched much porn. But as her eyes ate up Seth and Vaughn's show, she believed she was now a convert. They were a thing of beauty, and seeing Vaughn give up his iron-fisted control and submitting to his partner was a real turn-on.

She stepped into the room fully, pulling off pieces of clothing as she walked with a sway in her hips across the distance separating her and the boys. She saw Ronan's pupils dilate as they took in her appearance, but he made no move to come to her, instead he watched as she performed her mini strip tease. *Dirty voyeur,* she thought fondly. When she finally reached him, Ronan wrapped both his arms around her bare waist, bringing their bodies into full contact. He dipped his head, planting a chaste kiss on her lips.

"You okay?" he asked.

Her heart melted upon hearing the two softly spoken words. They were all naked, either highly aroused or already having sex, and yet the first words out of his mouth were concern for her emotional wellbeing. Was it any wonder she was in love with him?

"I'm fine. I'm with you," she answered truthfully.

The smile she received could have rivalled the sun in its intensity. Palming his face, she caressed his bottom lip with her thumbs. "I love you, Ronan."

His breath caught, and she thought she saw the suspicious sheen of tears in his lovely green eyes before he raised his hands to her face, mirroring her hold. "I love you, Ivory," he stated, copying her admission.

Joy burst inside her and she figured the wattage of her own smile must also be blinding. Leaning forwards, she kissed him with all the happiness bubbling inside of her – and a healthy dose of her lust as well, just for good measure. When they came up for air, they were both panting hard, with Seth and Vaughn's moans a lovely soundtrack behind them. She smiled up at Ronan one last time and turned around to watch her very own live porno.

Ronan wrapped his arms around her from behind, and although she could feel him hard and insistent at her back, he made no move to rectify his situation. "I suppose you love them too, huh?" he spoke lightly.

She grinned, adoring his playful side, happy that she could be free to be playful too. She sighed, nodding her head. "I'm afraid I do."

"Oh well. Considering I love them too, I can't fault your taste."

She laughed with happiness, enjoying the show on the bed in front of her until Seth's bandaged hand caught her attention and she remembered his terrible injury. Familiars healed fast, so it was already mending well. But it still worried her. "Should Seth really be quite so . . . vigorous?" she asked Ronan.

"He seems plenty fit to me. But let's see, shall we?" Ronan looped an arm around her waist and ushered her forwards. "Vaughn, does Seth seem fit enough to you?" he inquired, bending close enough to look into his lover's eyes.

Vaughn merely moaned in pleasure, Seth apparently hitting that secret spot inside him with what seemed like unerring accuracy and unrelenting force.

"I'd say Seth's managing just fine," Ronan decided, making her laugh. These guys were so much fun in the bedroom. She couldn't believe how lucky she was.

"I'm fine, babe." That was Seth's voice, now husky with desire. "But, if you want, you can always lend me another hand." He waggled his eyebrows suggestively.

She grinned but shook her head, palming Ronan's cock and eliciting a throaty groan from him. "My hands are full."

Seth *tsked*, slowing the movements of his hips and causing a disgruntled Vaughn to buck his own hips in objection. Seth merely slapped him on one well-toned arse cheek. "Patience," he chided.

And Ivory was definitely going to add spanking to her list of 'things to do in her harem.' The sound of Seth's palm making contact with Vaughn's butt? Capital H . . . O . . . T.

"You know, you're going to have to learn to multitask with three men to satisfy," Seth continued.

"Oh, am I just? And what if I think it's all of you who are going to have to learn to satisfy me?" She smirked, running a lazy hand over her breast, down her stomach, and into her own heat. Three distinct male groans were like music to her ears, and she smiled in triumph – for about a second – before she found herself airborne.

She landed with her lips conveniently close to Vaughn's and decided to take advantage, teasing them with her tongue. He opened instantly, and her desire ignited to flash point as their breath mingled and their tongues duelled.

To her surprise, Vaughn gentled the kiss, sipping and tasting rather than conquering, and she sighed in contentment. When they parted, the emotion in his eyes had the breath snagging in her throat. Having just seen the same look in Ronan's eyes, she recognised it for what it was: love. Her perpetually grumpy lover opened and closed his mouth silently, and she decided to cut him some slack. He was a man of few words at the best of times.

"I love you, Vaughn."

He nodded briskly, as if he knew all along, and followed it up with, "Ivory, I love you. So much." He jerked forwards again, kissing her passionately this time, and she gave herself up to the lust taking over her body once more.

Large hands spanned her waist, climbing higher before settling over her breasts. Calloused fingers plucked and squeezed at her right nipple even as wet heat engulfed her left. She pulled away from Vaughn's lips, moaning and gripping Ronan's hair in encouragement. He nibbled his way up to her neck, before sucking on the skin just under her ear. Ronan knew it was a hot spot for her and she felt her cat leaping to the surface at the contact. Kitty knew its mate was near and wanted to play.

Now that her glamour was no longer in place, the half of her that was familiar was very vocal. Her predator drive was strong, and the cat recognised its mates in the three male black jaguars in the room. As far as her animal was concerned, these males were hers and no-one else would ever do.

Wanting to play and needing to mark her territory once and for all, she allowed her claws to unsheathe and score lightly over Ronan's back. She didn't draw blood, but she was sure there would be long red streaks as a testament to her beast. A deep growl rumbled through her lover's chest, and she saw his pupils transform into vertical slits as his panther responded to its mate. He slipped his hands under her back and flipped her quickly and unceremoniously onto her stomach. She found herself with her butt high in the air and her shoulders pushed onto the giving mattress. She shivered when she recalled Ronan's words upon first learning they were mates; he wanted to mount her and sink his teeth into her. Oh boy, she sure hoped he was about to follow through.

Apparently, Seth also liked the idea because he withdrew from a complaining, cursing Vaughn, forcing him onto his hands and knees before holding him steady and plunging back into him in one smooth motion. Ivory ate up the sight, reaching out to run a hand through Vaughn's sweaty hair. He turned his face towards hers, smiling with his breath panting harshly, then his eyes flicked beyond her. A second later, warm hands stroked over her back from neck to rump, before Ronan's fingers found her core, testing her readiness. He needn't have bothered – she'd been drenched since she stepped into the doorway.

"Ronan, now," she begged, pushing her hips back and wiggling her arse provocatively from side to side.

One stinging slap to her left butt cheek had her crying out in surprise and desire. That felt good – too good – and she glanced over her shoulder at Ronan so he could see the pleasure in her gaze. He smirked a little, lodging the head of his cock at her entrance for one heart-stopping second before plunging into her heated depths. He set a demanding pace, and all she could do was grip the sheets beneath her and hang on for the ride. All too soon, she began to feel the telltale clenching of her womb and tingling in her clit.

Just a little bit more, she thought. Like magic, Ronan reached around, placing a heavy thumb on her clit and stroking firmly, even as she felt elongated canines sink into the flesh where her neck met her shoulder.

She detonated. There was no other word for it. She screamed, biting into the sheets, shuddering as her body clenched in a seemingly endless spasm of pleasure. Spots danced in front of her eyes – a series of snarls, groans, and roars meeting her ears as each man also became lost in the pleasure of the moment. She slumped onto the mattress, all strength eluding her. She received a soothing kiss between the shoulder blades from Ronan as he moved from behind her, and she murmured tiredly in thanks. Commanding her neck muscles to move, she watched Seth pull from Vaughn carefully, gently laying him down on a clean area of the sheets. They were a mess.

She gave about a second's thought to forcing them all into the shower, but Vaughn was already cuddling up beside Ronan where he had collapsed in a sated heap. The two had the goofy, satisfied looks of the well-fucked, and she didn't have the heart to chastise them for not cleaning up. The mattress dipped, and she saw Seth had returned with a couple of warm washcloths. He set about gently tidying up a snoozing Vaughn and a contented Ronan. Judging by the way neither man moved, she assumed this was a regular occurrence. Her Seth, the youngest of the three men and the most light-hearted, was also the most nurturing.

After he finished with the men, she allowed him to tend to her as well, opening her arms in welcome after he threw the washcloths back into the bathroom. He rolled her on top of him, apparently deciding she was going to be his blanket for the night. "Seth?"

"Hmm?"

"I love you."

His arms tightened around her and his breath stuttered from his chest. She raised her head, her jaguar allowing her to see just fine in the dark. His eyes were open and focused on hers – and he was smiling that same smile filled with love. "I love you too."

She kissed him, pouring out her passion and love and happiness. *Three for three. I got my trifecta. High five!* she mentally cheered.

"I love you too, Ronan. I love you, Vaughn," Seth

followed up, making sure his other lovers knew where they stood – always right beside him, Ivory knew.

"I love you too, Seth," Ronan replied from the darkness.

"Yes, yes. We all love each other. We're just one big happy fucking family. Now can you all shut up and go to sleep?"

Ivory's mouth dropped open for a moment before she laughed, sharing her amusement with Ronan and Seth. Vaughn sure did have a way with words.

Because they were, indeed, one big happy fucking family.

About the Author

ALL ABOUT MONTANA

Montana is an Aussie, self-confessed book junkie. She writes paranormal and urban fantasy romance with fun, sex, sarcasm, and magic. She has a soft spot for broody male leads that need a little redemption, and feisty female leads that can kick butt. Because Montana believes variety is the spice of life, she writes all kinds of relationships with all kinds of letters – MF, RH, and poly with MM. She is a scientist by day, a writer by night, and a reader always!

- Join her Facebook group here: Montana's Maniacs
- Email Montana here: montanaash.author@yahoo.com
- Visit her Website here: http://www.montanaash.com/
- Or check out the links below.

Also by Montana Ash

Montana has a chunk of books out in the wild, including multiple series, solo titles, boxsets, and co-written works.

For a full list of all of Montana's books, please check out her website:

http://www.montanaash.com/

Or seek her out on any of her social media platforms.

Or any book retailers.

She is everywhere!

Milton Keynes UK
Ingram Content Group UK Ltd.
UKHW020644070923
428220UK00012B/365